Tortured Justice

M. A. COMLEY

DEDICATION
This book is dedicated to my wonderful group of Facebook friends, you'll recognise your roles in the book I'm sure. Thanks for keeping me sane when I'm not wrapped up in writing my latest novel and killing off characters.

OTHER BOOKS BY
NEW YORK TIMES BEST SELLING AUTHOR
M. A. COMLEY

Cruel Justice

Impeding Justice

Final Justice

Foul Justice

Guaranteed Justice

Ultimate Justice

Virtual Justice

Hostile Justice

Tortured Justice

Rough Justice (coming Jan 2015)

Blind Justice (A Justice novella)

Evil In Disguise (Based on true events)

Torn Apart (Hero Series #1)

End Result (Hero Series #2)

Sole Intention (Intention Series #1)

Grave Intention (Intention Series #2)

Merry Widow (A Lorne Simpkins short story)

It's A Dog's Life (A Lorne Simpkins short story)

ACKNOWLEDGMENTS

As always love and best wishes to my wonderful Mum for the role she plays in my career. Special thanks to my superb editor Stefanie. Thanks also to Joseph my amazing proof reader.

Licence Notes.

TORTURED JUSTICE

PROLOGUE

The head of the group watched the other women arguing amongst themselves, frustrated that her well-thought-out plan appeared to be doomed from the outset. *What is wrong with you lot? I've spent months hatching this plan! Months!*

She clapped, calling for everyone's attention in the Griffin Hotel's conference room. She had booked the room at short notice because some of the women had complained they didn't have the time to drive out to the group's usual meeting place. Felicity had been cute when making the booking and used a fake name to avoid leaving a paper trail. "Keep the noise down to minimum, girls, as agreed. Right, have we decided?" Silence greeted her, and by the looks on the other members' faces it wasn't difficult to tell that in the past hour they had accomplished exactly nothing. She puffed out her cheeks as she sighed. "Okay, maybe we should just call the whole bloody thing off?"

"No! We can't do that." Julie stepped forward, towards Felicity. "I'll volunteer to go first, if you like."

Felicity acknowledged the woman's bravery with a smile. "That's settled then. The next question is: when should we carry out the deed? We need to be discreet, girls. The last thing we want to do is draw attention to ourselves. Not yet, not at this early stage. Any suggestions, Julie? You know him. We're at a disadvantage in that respect, we have no idea about his routine."

"Well, tonight would be an ideal opportunity. He usually goes to the pub on a Friday night around nine. Is that too soon to organise something?"

Felicity looked at the watch on her slender wrist and swept back a wisp of long blonde hair as she contemplated. "Well, it's seven o'clock now. I set up the other venue earlier just in case we came to a decision today to forge ahead with the plan. Let's take a vote on it, shall we? All those in favour of grabbing our first victim tonight, say I."

The I's were slow in coming much to Felicity's frustration. But eventually, after a few stragglers finally agreed, the plan was approved by the rest of the group. Her heart pounded; was that through fear or because of the excitement building within?

"Okay, let's get this plan sorted into some semblance of order. Julie, you say…" she paused and waited for her second-in-command to fill in the man's name.

"Don."

"Right, Don. Ah yes, I remember him well." Not personally, but she thought she had a fair idea of the pain and anguish the man had put her friend through over the years. It was time to rectify all those wrongs. *And tonight we're going to hand that punishment out, all of us.* That's what this group was about, righting the wrongs the men in each of the women's lives, had put them through over the years. "What pub?"

"The Horse and Cart."

"Okay, I need two more volunteers to accompany Julie and me this evening. The rest of you will go back to the other venue and wait for us."

The women chatted amongst themselves before Mags and Elaine raised their hands.

"Excellent. I have the weapons ready in the car."

"Weapons? No one said anything about using weapons," Elaine mumbled, fear lingering in her pale grey eyes.

Felicity folded her arms and tapped her foot. "How else do you expect us to overpower these men, Elaine? I'm all ears, hon?"

The woman gulped. "I suppose I hadn't really thought about that side of things."

Felicity raised her hand and pointed a finger at the crowd. "If anyone wants to back out, you need to speak up now. After tonight it will be too late to change things."

The other nine women shook their heads. Felicity couldn't help wondering how many of the women would regret agreeing to go ahead with the plan after the night was out. She thought the older women in the group would be the first to revolt after they captured Don.

For the next half an hour they wrote out the details of the attack in full and thirty minutes after that the group split up. Six of the ladies jumped into two cars and headed back to the cottage, while Julie, Mags, and Elaine joined their leader in the car and drove to the Horse and Cart, where they awaited their prey.

Julie pointed at a silver Mondeo which cruised to a halt at the rear of the car park. Fortunately, the car park was pretty quiet for this time of night, especially on a Friday due to the local football team holding their annual awards dinner at the community centre down the road. Don left his vehicle and walked towards the car the ladies were hiding in close to the entrance of the pub.

"Get ready, girls. Julie, you get out of the car first and strike up a conversation with him. Can you do that?"

Julie shrugged and her mouth twisted. "Oh my! I'm not sure."

"It's too late to have second thoughts now," Mags snarled in the back seat. "Get a grip, woman and get out there."

"Thank you, Mags, less of the anger."

"Sorry. Come on, Julie. We have one shot at this," Mags stated, offering her friend a smile.

Julie let out an exasperated breath and hooked her hand around the door handle. "Wish me luck."

"Good luck," the three girls responded. Felicity reached down beside her and pulled out the cricket bat. It was the only weapon she could lay her hands on at her home; everything else was at the cottage. She squinted as she watched Julie take slow, hesitant steps towards the man who'd made her life hell throughout their ten-year marriage. Don's pace never faltered as he neared his ex-wife but his face contorted with rage. "Get ready, girls, I'm not liking the way he's greeting her."

Julie tried to stand in her ex's path but he brushed her slight frame aside. The car doors opened at the same time and the three occupants formed a line in front of the shocked man. His eyes drifted down to the bat Felicity was tapping in the palm of her hand.

"What's going on here? Get out of my way?" He spun around and shouted at Julie. "Are you behind this?"

Julie stormed forward and slapped her ex hard around the face. "Yes, meet my friends. They'd like a little chat with you."

Before he had the chance to respond, Felicity swiped the bat, aiming at his head. The man tottered unsteadily in place. Another blow with the bat forced him down on the ground. The girls launched, attacking him with their weapons. A high-heeled shoe stabbed him in the upper leg. Another blunt instrument in the shape of a stunted iron bar came crashing down on his forearm. Everyone in the group heard the bone snap and Don cried out in pain.

"Stop! I'll get you for this, Julie, if it's the last thing I do." He cried out again, his injured arm clutched the top of his other arm as the pain increased on his face. He gasped for breath and whimpered,

"Help me, the pain… I need to go to the hosp…" his voice trailed off as the women continued to beat him.

A few seconds later, Julie called a halt to the attack. "Stop. That's enough. We want him alive, don't we? What's the pleasure in killing him now, we need him to *really* suffer."

The four women looked around them, then stared down at the man writhing in agony on the tarmac at their feet.

"We didn't hit him that much. What's wrong with him?" Mags asked bewildered.

Julie gasped and her hand flew up to cover her mouth.

Felicity took a step toward her, confused by her friend's reaction. "What? What is it, Julie?"

"Damn, I forgot."

"Forgot what?" Felicity demanded.

"He has a bad heart."

"Crap, now you tell me?" Felicity paced the immediate area as she thought and clicked her fingers when she came up with a solution. "Okay, let's get him in the car."

"Why?" Julie asked.

"We'll drop him off near the hospital."

The four women each grabbed a limb and bundled the groaning man into the back of the car. Felicity jumped in the driver's seat and revved the engine while the others strapped on their seatbelts. "Ready? Keep an eye on him, he might be pulling a fast one."

"I doubt that, his lips are turning blue. Hurry!" Julie replied, unmistakable panic in her voice.

Felicity put her foot down, the car sped out of the car park and headed towards the hospital. The only sound in the car was the increasing moans of their victim. The vehicle came to an abrupt halt in the street just around the corner from the hospital entrance. "Okay, let's get him out."

Julie gasped again. "My God, you can't leave him here. We have to take him to A&E. If he dies what will happen to us then?"

"Stop panicking, Julie, he's not going to die." Felicity got out of the car and opened the back door. Mags jumped out and together they heaved the victim from the vehicle. He fell to the ground amidst more grunts and groans. "Get back in, Mags."

Felicity sped away from the scene at seventy miles an hour, taking a cursory glimpse in the rear-view mirror at the pain-riddled man they'd left lying on the ground, uncertain if he'd just taken his final breath or not.

CHAPTER ONE

"How could someone do such a thing?" Lorne raked a hand through her shoulder-length hair. The dog with the sorrowful brown eyes stared up at her.

"Mum, we can worry about that later. We need to get this poor girl to the vet, quickly."

Lorne bent down to stroke the petrified creature, which couldn't have been more than a year old. A thinning layer of hair covered her trembling, sore-covered body, obviously suffering from demodectic mange. Thankfully, her four pups appeared to be faring better than she was, even if they were a little underweight. Some callous bastard had dumped the five dogs down by the boating lake twenty minutes away, leaving the pups tied up in a black bag. Getting the dog into the car had been a mammoth task because the mother was understandably terrified of people. Lorne cautiously held out a hand for the dog to sniff, and the bitch turned her head away. Lorne felt as though a knife had pierced her heart. No dog had ever avoided her like that.

Standing up, she flung an arm around Charlie's shoulder. "You're right, off to the vet we go. I'll go ring him to let him know we're on our way. Why don't you try and gain a bit of trust with her, eh?"

"Okay. Looking at her, that's going to take an eternity. I'll try and give her some food. She looks like she hasn't eaten in weeks."

"I'll be right back." Lorne left the kennel at the rescue centre she ran with her family. Well, actually the job of running the place was now safely in the hands of her husband, Tony, and her daughter, Charlie. Although she'd returned to the Met a year ago, she still found it impossible to stay away from the centre, especially when a case as deplorable as this came their way. Mercifully, not many cases as bad as this one passed through their doors. However, when they did, Lorne despised the human beings who would dream of treating an animal, any animal, in such a horrendous way. She could see no reason for it. Any form of animal abuse was uncalled for, in her eyes. No one ever *forced* anyone to give a dog a home. Lorne was saddened and infuriated by the weekly reports of just how many dogs were being dumped in shelters across the country. Whatever happened to that saying, 'A dog is for life, not just for Christmas'?

Surely nowadays, there were enough programmes on the TV telling people how much daily exercise a dog needed. Were people really dumb enough to think a dog would be happy stuck in a backyard, often no larger than a postage stamp, all their lives? How would they feel to live such a pitiful existence?

"Hey, you. What's with the frown?" Tony stepped forward and kissed her on the lips.

"I'm sorry, hon. I'm internally ranting about how stupid the human race can be regarding animals, better internally than chewing your ear off all the time, eh?" She smiled and picked up the phone. "I have to ring the vet. I'll go with Charlie while you carry on with the morning chores if you like?"

"What about your own job, are you forgetting that, love?"

Lorne grimaced. Yes, she had temporarily forgotten about it. "Oops, should I ring in sick?"

"That's up to you. Knowing your conscience the way I do, it wouldn't be happy with that scenario. Why don't you trust Charlie and me to take the dogs to the vet and you get ready to start your *proper* job?"

"You're right. You're always right. Let me at least make the appointment for you. The mother dog might have to be separated from her pups for a while until she recovers. I've never seen such a bad case of mange. I don't think the pups have been affected yet, but who's to say what those little parasites are up to; they jump from animal to animal undetected most of the time."

"Let's not get ahead of ourselves just yet. Let's see what the vet's test results come back first. What if he wants to keep her overnight or for a few days?"

Lorne thought over the proposal thoroughly before responding. "I'm not averse to that, there will be a cost implication involved though. Unless..."

"Unless? What are you hatching?"

"Just plead poverty. Make sure the vet knows how many strays we're caring for at the moment, lay it on thick if you have to."

"You're impossible, woman. I'll be sure to let him know. Make the call and get ready for work." He tapped her on the backside and winked.

Half an hour later a reluctant Lorne drove into work, having made the appointment with the vet for eleven that morning. It was at times like this she really missed being her own boss and caring for the dogs who needed her help on a daily basis, not that she didn't trust Charlie or Tony to look after the animals well, of course. In her eyes, no one cared for the dogs as much as she could. However, necessity had forced her back to her role in the force, both financially and for her own sanity. She had struggled with the concept of giving up the daily grind of chasing criminals after ten years on the force; even starting up her own private investigator business with Tony hadn't satisfied that hunger.

So, there she was driving into work, a detective sergeant in the team she used to run, which was now under the leadership of her former DS and good friend, Katy Foster. At first, Lorne had felt awkward taking orders from Katy, not that she issued many anyway. Katy had reassured her that everything would turn out fine. On her first day back on the force Katy had taken her to one side to ensure her that she would be treated as a proper partner, an equal. It made complete sense considering Lorne's wealth of experience. They were like-minded women and so far their partnership had been a huge success which had come as no surprise to Sean Roberts, their DCI, who had begged Lorne for months to return to his team.

She drew up alongside Katy's car in the station car park. Her partner was sitting inside her car having what looked to be a fraught conversation with someone on her mobile phone. Seeing Lorne, she rolled her eyes and intimated with a raised finger that she would be another minute or so. A few seconds later Katy's door sprung open.

"Trouble?"

Katy shook her head. "Not really, just strife from Mum and Dad for not visiting them in months. When are they going to realise that I live a very stressful life and that I now live almost one hundred and fifty miles from them? I can't just drop everything and take off for the weekend."

They walked through the main entrance of the station and up the flight of stairs that led to the incident room they called their second home. "They miss you. Try and see it from their point of view, hon."

"I know. It's hard for all of us. I'll put my thinking cap on and see if there's a way I can get them down here to visit me soon."

"That's a great idea! You could buy one of those West End packages. They could go see a few shows and stay in a plush hotel."

Katy snorted. "Steady on there, I ain't made of money."

"Oops, yeah I totally forgot what a detective inspector's wage is. Mind you, it's a darn sight better than what I'm on."

"Point taken. How's Charlie and Tony?"

They stopped at the vending machine to buy two cups of coffee and proceeded into the office. "Fine. They're on a mission today. We had a sorry-looking boxer arrive yesterday. I made an appointment at the vet for later on this morning. The poor dog has got the worst bout of mange I've ever seen. Her owner dumped her. How can people disown a dog like that?"

"Eww… is it really bad? I mean I've seen some awful cases with dogs suffering from that on the TV."

"Yeah, it's horrendous. Her skin is just one large patch of sores, either red raw or full of crusty skin. At least the pups seem to have escaped it, so far."

"What? She has pups? That's terrible, Lorne."

"Yeah, four of them. I reckon they're no older than about four weeks old. We got a call from a member of the public about a dog clawing at a black bag. When Tony and I shot down there we found the pups tied up in a black bag."

Katy gasped. "Poor things. What a shitty start to life they've had."

"I'm hoping we can change that. I sense the vet's bill being extremely high though."

They were interrupted by a knock on the door. AJ poked his head into the room and gave Katy one of his special smiles, which didn't go unnoticed by Lorne. She supressed the urge to giggle and wished the couple would admit they had feelings for each other and get on with having a good time. The flipside of that notion was that if they came out of the closet, so to speak, they would no longer be able to work on the same team whilst both employed by the Met. It just wasn't appropriate behaviour for serving officers.

"Hi, AJ. What's up?" Katy asked, her professional etiquette clear to see.

"We've got a body, ma'am. Out near the hospital, it was discovered a few hours ago."

"Okay, male or female? And is the pathologist aware of the discovery?" Katy asked, taking a sip of her coffee.

Lorne did the same as she listened to the conversation. She had a feeling the few sips of coffee she managed to slurp down now would be all they had time for the rest of the morning.

"Male, and yes, the pathologist is on site."

"Thanks, AJ. We'll set off shortly."

AJ left the office and the two women gulped down a few extra sips of coffee before they followed him out.

Katy addressed her team of detectives. "Okay, hopefully Lorne and I won't be too long. Busy yourselves with finishing up the paperwork for the crimes we completed last week in the meantime, folks. Just in case this victim comes with a lot of baggage that needs solving promptly."

All four detectives nodded and got back to work.

Lorne and Katy made their way over to the screened off area, produced their IDs and ducked under the tape. "Hi, Patti. Are you close to finishing up?" Lorne asked.

"Yep, I'm just about done. It's not as cut and dried as I first thought," the pathologist replied, studying the body from a few feet away.

"In what way?" asked Katy, glancing sideways at Lorne, as if to say, 'here we go again.'

"Well, at first I presumed—I know, never presume—the gentleman had simply suffered a heart attack. But upon further inspection, it looks like he received a whack to the neck and head, as well." Patti crouched and pointed out the specific areas affected then shuffled along the body to the man's legs. "However, this injury here seems to be the origin of what has actually caused his death. I'll be able to determine more back at the mortuary, when I have a naked specimen before me. Will you ladies be joining me?"

Katy shrugged. "Why not, we've got nothing better to do. Any idea when the PM will be?"

"I'm pretty clear today. If you follow me back I can get started right away."

"Wow, that's unheard of for you, Patti. Is crime that much down in the area, at present?" Lorne smiled and raised an expectant eyebrow.

"Hardly, I've just been given an associate to work with. He's pretty keen to lighten my load at the moment while I get on with sorting through my mountain of paperwork. Some of which is almost six months behind."

"Well, it's about time the department gave you some extra help. Fit is he?" Katy winked as she asked the question.

"Fit as in physically fit, yes, apparently he works out at the gym at least four times a week, so he says. Fit as in would I give him one? Well, let's just say if I were twenty years younger I'd have taken him on one of the examination tables on his first day."

The three women roared with laughter; it wasn't uncommon to lighten the mood at a scene and crack a joke. If they didn't they'd all go nuts.

"Patti, you're a married woman for goodness sake," Lorne said, taking in the scene once more.

"You forgot the happily married part. Yes, but it doesn't mean I can't keep an eye on what's going on around me, you did with Tony."

Lorne's eyes widened and her mouth dropped open much to her friend's amusement. "Excuse me?"

"I remember you telling me that all it took was a quick jaunt to France and bingo bango!" Patti went on, adding to Lorne's embarrassment.

"*Bingo-bango*? Good grief, woman. I think you've been working in that mortuary too much. You need to get out into the real world more often. And FYI, my marriage to Tom was over long before I started any *funny* business with Tony, just saying."

Katy sniggered, and Lorne turned to look at her.

"Stop encouraging her. Now that we've dissected my relationship with my husband—or should that be *husbands*?—can we get back to the case in hand?"

Patti smiled. "Ah avoidance tactics! Yes, okay. I'm finished here, why don't I get my people to load up the body and we'll make our way back to the mortuary?"

Lorne sensed the pathologist, her good friend, striking an imaginary finger in the air, marking a win for herself. She would need to come up with an idea of how to get her revenge for that uncalled for ridicule.

CHAPTER TWO

Suited and booted in the appropriate uniform fit for a post mortem, Lorne and Katy walked into the examination room with Patti to find the victim was already in situ, ready awaiting the pathologist's knife.

Lorne and Katy watched Patti search the man's naked body, looking for any other external injuries before she cut him open. "Yep, this definitely contributed to his death."

The detectives leaned over the corpse. "Odd shape. It's not a knife wound is it?" Lorne asked, glancing sideways at Patti who shook her head.

"Nope, that would be more like a slit in the skin. This is more like a puncture wound."

Frowning, Lorne asked, "From what?"

Patti retrieved her measure from the movable trolley and placed it on the wound to obtain the length and width of the opening. "Well, if I didn't know any better I'd say it came from a woman's shoe, a stiletto to be more precise."

"Really?" Katy moved in for a closer look. "A stiletto can do that much damage?"

"It only really needed to puncture the skin. It was the accuracy of the blow that caused the real damage—it struck the main artery. An inch to the left or right, and this man probably would have survived. Of course, the heart attack might have ended up killing him, but he would've had a greater chance of survival. The blood at the scene told me he bled out from this wound, which makes sense, considering the heel connected with the artery. The fact that the body lay undiscovered for a good few hours after the attack was also a contributing factor in his death."

Lorne studied the wound for a second or two. "So, are you saying that the wound was intentional? As in, we should be out there looking for a murderer? Or could this simply have been an unfortunate accident?"

Patti raised an eyebrow. "An unfortunate accident? The person probably had to take her shoe off to cause the wound, Lorne. I'd say that was an intentional act, wouldn't you?"

"Sorry. That came out like a dumb conclusion. So you're saying the victim would have been upright when struck, not lying on the floor? What I was thinking was that maybe the perpetrator could have stamped on the man's leg while he was on the floor."

"That's plausible. Hey look, at this point, I'm just giving you the facts. It's down to you to find out the whys and wherefores."

Lorne shrugged. "It helps if we have an inkling, Patti. Maybe this was just an accident after all."

"Hmm… not too keen on that idea, Lorne," Katy said. "I don't know about you, but in all my years of wearing high-heels, the thought has never occurred to me to use one of my shoes as a weapon."

"Extenuating circumstances, possibly? Perhaps the man tried to rape the woman? You'd reach for anything available to try and fend off an attack, wouldn't you?"

"She has a valid point, Katy. I know if I were in such a perilous situation, I would slip off a shoe and whack the bastard before he even thought about attacking me." Patti picked up her scalpel and inserted it into the man's flesh, ready to make the Y-cut that would allow her to peel back the man's flesh to expose his organs.

Lorne and Katy both turned their heads and walked over to the side of the room.

"We'll hang around here for another half an hour or so and then get on with the investigation. We have the man's bank card, we can use that to track down his address as that's all he seemed to have on him. I'll get AJ to do a background check too, maybe he's got a record for sexual assault charges or something along those lines, it'll be a start anyway," Katy said, taking charge of the investigation as any detective inspector would.

"Agreed. I don't think we need to stay around here longer than necessary, Patti has already told us what the cause of death is in her opinion. The quicker we get things started the more chance we have of capturing the culprit. Seems a little unbelievable that a woman's shoe caused his death though, doesn't it?"

"Put it this way—nothing surprises me anymore in this game."

Patti concluded her findings and reiterated her first assumption of how the victim, Don Alder had died. Initial bleeding from the artery had led to a major heart attack, although the heart attack, at least the start of one, might have come first. Lorne and Katy left the mortuary and headed back to the station.

Katy handed AJ the bank card. "AJ, the victim had this in his wallet, nothing else. Track down his address, if you will?"

She and Lorne went through to the office.

"What do you want me to do?" Lorne asked.

"Once AJ has the address, we'll head out. In the meantime, see what you can dig up about the victim. No—wait a minute. Let AJ do that while we're out. Can you start filling in the details on the investigation board?"

"Of course, although there won't be much to fill in, apart from the man's name and the scene of the crime—oh, and the suspected weapon."

Katy nodded. "That'll do, for starters. I'll be out once I've been through the post. If I don't make a start, you know what it's like."

"Yep, definitely one part of the job I don't envy you having to deal with daily. Oh, can I ring home before I begin, to check on how Tony got on at the vet's?"

"Go for it. Let me know what the outcome was."

Lorne rang home once she returned to the incident room. Tony answered after the second ring. "Hi, how did you get on with the vet?"

"You were right in your assessment—she has mange. The good news is that it's treatable. We can aid her recovery here, the vet said. No need for him to keep her in. The pups had a clean bill of health, which was a relief."

"That's fantastic news. Did the vet give her an antibiotic injection?"

"Yep, we've got to give her a course of tablets, too. Here's the funny thing: he also told me to put a T-shirt on her."

"That's right, to stop her from scratching. Can you imagine the irritation to her skin? It's red raw, Tony. Grab one of my old crop tops from the chest of drawers. That should be large enough to cover most of the affected area."

"Will do. I need to give her a shower first—the vet gave me a special shampoo. It's warm at the moment. Shall I stick her in that metal tub and use the hose on her?"

Lorne smiled at her husband's practical side. "Get Charlie to bathe her. Tell her to grab a pair of my latex gloves and use a bucket of tepid water to wash her. Then she can be hosed off. Okay?"

"Yes, boss. How are things at your end?"

"New case just dropped on the table, still in the early stages. It looks like we can call this case death by a stiletto."

Tony chuckled. "Sorry, I shouldn't laugh, but it does sound funny. Good luck with that one. Have you identified the victim?"

"Yes. Less concern about my job, hon. You just concentrate on getting that little lady in your care sorted. We need to think up a name for her, too. We'll let Charlie do that, shall we?"

"Okay, enough nattering. We both have jobs to do. I'll see you later."

"Tony, wait. Before you hang up, dare I ask how much the bill was?"

"Umm... I was hoping you wouldn't ask. We'll talk about it later, yes?"

"No. We'll discuss it now. Go on, hit me with it."

"A little over two hundred," Tony mumbled.

"What? You're pulling my leg, aren't you?"

"Afraid not, love. I pleaded poverty, and he retorted that *we* might be running a charity, but he wasn't."

"Wow, what a pig. I think we need to start looking around for another vet, pronto. Remind me to ring Sue at the RSPCA later, see if she can recommend one. That's outrageous."

"It's the medication. He was kind enough to waive his consultation fee for me."

"Big deal. Okay, speak later. Thanks for taking her, Tony."

"No problem. Enjoy the rest of your day."

Lorne hung up. She shook her head, wondering where on earth she was going to come up with enough money to keep the rescue centre afloat. Maybe she should consider robbing a bank to get her out of the fix.

"Penny for them?" AJ sat on the edge of her desk.

"It'll cost you more than that to find out what I'm thinking, AJ. Did you get the man's address?"

"Yep. He lives in a flat about ten minutes from here, 10 Hyde Lane."

"Brilliant. While Katy and I are out, can you delve into his background, find out the usual? Whether he has any record or previous convictions? It seems odd that this could be considered a random attack."

"I'll dig deep, see what I can find. Everything all right? You look a little upset."

"Yeah, bad news regarding a vet's bill. I'll overcome it somehow. I usually do. Thanks for asking." She leaned forward and whispered, "How are things going with you and Katy?"

Lorne's partner came out of her office, eyes firing daggers in her direction.

"Er, never mind. Forget I asked."

"Lorne? Ready are we?"

"We are, ma'am. Thanks for the info, AJ." She rose from her chair, collected her handbag, and left the incident room after Katy.

"I know what you were up to back there," her partner called over her shoulder, descending the stairs ahead of her.

"Don't know what you mean. AJ gave me the man's address and was enquiring how things were at home. That's all."

"Yeah, right! I've told you before never to underestimate me, Lorne. I had a good teacher, remember?"

"The dog's going to be fine. Thanks for asking," she said, changing the subject while making a face behind her friend's back.

"Glad to hear it. I hope the wind doesn't get up and set that expression in place, hon." Katy swiftly turned to look at her, grinning broadly.

Lorne blinked furiously. "Don't know what you mean. I'm innocent of all charges laid at my door."

"Hmm... let's get to this man's address before I punch your lights out for insubordination."

"Ooo... big word. I prefer porridge in the mornings. Not keen on swallowing a dictionary first thing."

"Smartarse."

Once settled in Katy's car, Lorne punched the man's address into the sat nav and waited for the directions to appear. Then they set off and pulled up outside the man's flat about ten minutes later. The ground-floor flat was part of a terraced house. They got no answer when they tried the victim's bell, so Lorne buzzed the upstairs flat.

A groggy male voice answered, "Yeah? What do you want? Some of us are trying to get some sleep here."

"Police, open up, please. We'd like to ask you a few questions about your neighbour."

The man grumbled as if chatting to someone in the flat with him.

Lorne's brow furrowed.

Katy pressed the bell again and held the button down until the man shouted at her to stop.

"Cut it out. I'll get dressed and come down. Give me a sec."

Katy tutted. "Make it quick. We haven't got all day, mate."

Another two minutes passed before a scruffy young man wearing a T-shirt and jeans opened the door.

Katy and Lorne produced their IDs and waved them in his face. He looked either drunk or stoned still from the previous night's activities.

"Mr. Don Alder, what can you tell us about him?"

"Why? Is he in some kind of bother? I knew he was hiding something, the crafty old git."

"Meaning what?"

"He just seems a little shifty. Always looks down his nose at me when I meet him on the doorstep here, not that I have much to do with him."

"Shifty? In what sort of way?"

"I don't know. I ain't no copper. What's he done?"

Katy blew out a breath that moved her fringe. "He's dead."

The young man stumbled backwards into the front door. "What?"

"We're eager to get on with our investigation, Mr...?"

"Callum. Eric Callum."

"Mr. Callum, can you tell us if Mr. Alder lived alone?"

"He does—or did, yes. His wife left him about a year ago, I think."

"Okay, I don't suppose you have a contact address for her, do you?" Katy asked.

"Nope. I'm nobody's keeper."

"There's no need for sarcasm, Mr. Callum."

"I was just stating a fact. I think he had a sister, too. Not sure where she lives, either, so don't bother asking me."

"Any idea of her name? Anything you can tell us will help, no matter how insignificant you think it might be."

The man shrugged and scratched his head as he thought. "Nope, can't help. I think she was local, although I can't be sure about that. Sorry."

"When was the last time you saw Mr. Alder?" Lorne asked, sensing the meeting was about to come to a close.

"Last week. He was alive and kicking then, all right. Complained about the noise when I had a party. He was always moaning about something."

Lorne asked, "Do you know where we can get a key to his flat? Have you got the landlord's phone number?"

"Just a sec. I'll get it for you." The man left them waiting on the doorstep and returned with a scrap of paper with a number written on it. He gave the information to Katy.

"Thanks. One last thing before we leave you to get back to bed. Did you ever hear any disturbances coming from the flat? You know, in the form of arguments?"

His mouth turned down as he searched his memory. "Can't remember anything… all has been quiet since his wife left."

"You've been really helpful," Katy replied.

"What are you thinking?" Lorne asked as they walked back to the car.

"That we need to track down Mrs. Alder."

"Well, it's a possibility she's involved because of the weapon used in his death. We can't rule her out, especially if they had a troubled relationship, can we?" Lorne opened the door to the car and got in.

"I was thinking along the same lines. Next stop—the landlord, to see if he has another address for the wife," Katy said.

"I doubt he'll have that if they separated acrimoniously, but he may be able to give us her name."

Katy pulled away and drove back to the station. The team spent the rest of the afternoon trying to find information that would lead them to the name of the victim's wife or sister. They had to find at least one of them if they were going to crack the case.

Lorne headed home, feeling weary after being embroiled in a frustrating afternoon when clues had proved virtually impossible to find. The landlord was away until the following week, and no one at his office had a key to his personal files. *Nothing like trusting your staff while you up and leave the country.*

Tony met her in the drive with a welcome cuddle and a long kiss. "I needed that. How's the dog? Has Charlie named her yet?"

"As a matter of fact, yes, she has. Onyx."

"I like it. It suits her. Let's go and see her."

"I popped in about an hour ago and she seems fine. No laughing when you see her."

Arms around each other's waist they walked into the kennels. Lorne opened the kennel where Onyx was lying on her padded bed, her pups feeding happily on her teats. "Aww, how cute. Instinct has made them search out her teats under the T-shirt. It looks better on her than it ever did on me." Lorne chuckled and bent down to stroke Onyx's head. Her tail wagged tentatively at first but sped up when she realised Lorne meant her and her puppies no harm. "It's all right, sweetie. We're going to help you get over this. I know it's hard to trust humans after the way you've been treated in the past; we'll do our best to right that wrong."

"Charlie is fond of her already. I sense another tussle coming your way."

"She's got to learn to toughen up. She'd want all the rescue dogs living here permanently if she had her way. I'm going to ring the local TV station, see if they can help us find a new home for her, I think she's such a deserving case. I'd also like to see if anyone recognises her, maybe someone will snitch on her owner. It would be great if we could slap an animal cruelty charge on them."

"Good idea. Let's see if the treatment works first. Although, to me, just having that one bath, her skin seems to be less irritated. Charlie has to bathe her every day for the next week or so. Then we have to take her back to the vet for another check-up."

"That's great that there has been an improvement so far. The injection probably helped, too. Let's hope the vet doesn't charge for the follow-up visit. He shouldn't, but that's not always the case. You get better soon, girl. We'll ensure you receive all the love you need to fight this and give you the strength to find a happy forever home."

"Come on, you big softie. Let's get you fed and watered. I think Charlie mentioned she was off out tonight, so we'll have the house to ourselves. I'm going to cook steak and chips for tea."

"Mind if I cook tea? I feel like doing a mundane domestic chore for a change."

"Sure. I'm not going to stand in your way. I'll put my feet up and watch the World Cup, suits me."

Lorne chuckled. "Now that England have been knocked out, there's sure to be a good match on. Did Charlie say who she was going out with?"

"Stop frowning. You need to learn to trust her again. Wendy's death was an unfortunate accident that she tried to prevent."

"I know. She's my baby, though. It's hard seeing her grow up and making her own decisions in life."

"True. You're not alone there. I'm sure every mother throughout the world goes through the same dilemma when their own children cut the apron strings, hon."

Lorne closed the kennel door and kissed her husband. "For someone who has never had kids of their own, you understand a father's role impeccably."

"I've been watching and learning from you. You might think you come down hard on Charlie, but you don't. Not all teenagers have the freedom you allow her. She appreciates that, too. She might not say as much, but I know she does."

Lorne's heart melted at the smile on his face and his cherished words. She was lucky to have found such a sensitive man. Who knew former MI6 operatives had it in them to be such gentle souls?

CHAPTER THREE

Sitting in her comfy Queen Anne chair positioned next to the fire which on a winter's nights she found comforting, Felicity thought over the next part of her cunning plan. She made copious notes and referred back to the dozens she'd already made and altered numerous times over the past few months. Excitement mounted within, gnawing at her nerve endings when she thought about the different types of torture out there. Torture that she could apply to their victims, hoping that none of them ended up having a heart attack like Don Alder had. Reading about his demise in the newspaper left her feeling dissatisfied beyond words. His death hadn't been painful enough. She had wanted him to suffer so much more, through long and sustained misery, for the way he'd treated Julie for years. The hardship she had suffered needed compensation, but the idiot couldn't handle the pain, even as minimal as it had been.

Felicity had been forced to rethink her plans and choose a much younger man for their next victim, one who would be able to endure hours of endless pain. The worthy man was Jordan Calleja, a native from Malta who had arrived in England and married Dara after meeting her on holiday ten years ago. Dara's reluctance to get Jordan involved in the group's venture had annoyed Felicity, so much so that she intended to heap even more punishment on the man.

She hated being questioned by any member of the group. It was imperative that she show her authority in ways that shocked and kept the other members in line. She had a list of torture techniques lined up for Jordan, and by the end of it, he would be putty in her hands, willing to do *anything* to save himself from further pain and possible loss of limbs.

Dara was foolish for still loving him, in spite of all his failings. He'd cheated on her with several women and had even had the audacity to go back home to tell her. Taking pride in making comparisons with her, he hadn't held back on telling her the gruesome details of all his extramarital sexual encounters. Dara had turned up at one of the group's weekly book club meetings, distraught and inconsolable. It was then that the other women had spoken out about the flaws in their own relationships, which, in turn, had caused Felicity to reflect on the damage her own husband had caused to her marriage and family unit. But her own gratification would wait until all the other women in the group had seen their menfolk either punished or killed. After Dara's revelation, the group had evolved and branched off in a different direction, once each of them had shared her deepest inner thoughts. In the past, Felicity had been known to experiment with the odd spell or two, but recently, she had delved much deeper into the darker side of witchcraft, unbeknownst to the rest of the group.

Her next task after choosing a victim had been to call a group meeting. She hoped to persuade them to meet up later that evening. There were bound to be a few who couldn't attend—the group had agreed that the majority votes would be honoured in all decision making even when the entire group was not present.

By the end of the hour, she had succeeded in ringing and persuading eight other group members to join her at the cottage buried deep in the woods, at ten p.m. After dressing in her leadership robe, she jumped in the car and sped to the cottage. First to arrive, she lit all the candles in the sconces around the exterior of the room and the chandelier in the centre near the altar. This was where she belonged. She let out a deep, satisfying sigh and swirled around. Whenever she visited her parents' former home, tucked away down a small country lane, away from prying eyes, she had an overwhelming feeling of freedom.

One by one, the women arrived and slipped into their costumes. Felicity studied them with a sense of pride trickling through her veins. She loved each woman like a sister, the sister her mother had lost during birth forty years ago. All of them were very different in character, some far stronger than others. It was the weaker ones in the group who caused Felicity more concern than she could handle at times. She knew that their characters would be tested and stretched to new limits over the coming weeks, and she had no way of knowing if her plans would end up biting her in the backside. All she knew was how important it was *not* to let men think they could get one over on these women. There had to be boundaries in life no man should ever cross. Men needed to recognise equality in life and that without the female gender, the human race just wouldn't exist. That snippet of knowledge never occurred to men while they were thrashing the living daylights out of women or putting them down to their mates over a pint of beer down the pub.

The women joined hands in a circle around the altar, and the chanting began, quietly at first. As the chanting escalated to a noisy crescendo, the women raised their arms above their heads. Felicity said the final words, and everyone cheered and applauded, calling the meeting to commence.

Felicity surveyed the crowd of anxious faces before her. "Right, our plan has progressed onto Stage Two, the second victim. Unfortunately, Julie was too distraught to attend our gathering tonight after what happened to Don. I've assured her our hearts and thoughts are with her at this sad time. His death was a regrettable accident, and one that we hope won't ever happen again. Nevertheless, it will *not* stop us from carrying out our mission. These men need to be taught a lesson, once and for all. We will capture our next victim tomorrow. I've chosen this subject personally without a vote. You *will* have to trust my decision this time around. We cannot have another incident such as the one that happened to Don. It will only raise suspicions in the outside world. Therefore, I'm nominating Jordan Calleja to be the next person on our list."

Several gasps spread through the crowd, and all eyes landed on Dara. Her mouth fell open, and her legs momentarily gave way as the colour swiftly drained from her usually rosy cheeks. Kaz and Sally grabbed an arm each, preventing her from falling.

"No... you can't. I want to back out. I don't want Jordan to suffer."

Felicity took three steps and stopped inches in front of the protesting woman. Dara's gaze drifted off to the left. The blood pumping through her veins felt as if it were on a mission from hell, the heat intensifying during its journey. However, she didn't let her anger show outwardly, not yet. Smiling, she said, "Dara, we agreed from day one that no one would back out."

"I know... but that was then. After what happened to Don, I've changed my mind. It's not fair that our menfolk should suffer like this, be tormented by our hands."

She turned on her heel and paced before the assembled crowd. "Let me put it this way, Dara. All of you, do you seriously think your ex-partners, any of them, stopped to consider your feelings before they struck you or treated you like shit? Do you?" Her voice rose, and she mentally kicked herself for getting irate. She hadn't intended to let that show, not yet.

"There's no need for this anger. We're all rid of these men now. Why can't we leave it that way? Why do we have to set out on this course of destruction?" Dara asked, still flanked by her two friends.

Felicity halted and approached the weak link in the group again. "Is that what you want? Seriously? To brush all those hours of pain and anguish under the carpet as though it never happened?"

Dara nodded slowly, her eyes cast down at the ground. "Yes." The word left her trembling lips as nothing more than a whisper.

Felicity studied the woman for a long moment then shrugged and returned to the altar. "Well, that's not what you signed up for, Dara, or any of you. The plan has already been set in motion, and there's no going back, either now or in the near future." Dara glanced around at the other women in the room, and Felicity, for the first time since the group had formed a year ago, felt the stirrings of revolt from the other members. She had to prevent it from escalating further. *But how?* Were the women really that gutless? All the talk during their meetings for the past month or so had consisted of what each individual wanted to do to the man who had wronged her so much. After one minor voice of dissent, she sensed the whole proposal was doomed before it even had the chance to get off the ground. Seeing the way Don had suffered had gripped her in a wonderfully thrilling way. She had gone to bed that night, revelling in the man's discomfort as the scene replayed over and over in her mind. She craved hearing the men cry out for forgiveness.

She shook her head. "Maybe we should vote on whether we ought to continue this or not? Be warned, though, if you want to back out this time, there will never be another opportunity to return to the scheme. I have better things to do with my time than spend hours—no days, coming up with the procedures we need to exact our revenge, only for a lone voice to cry out and say, 'Stop, you can't do that to my man.' Make your decision quickly, ladies. I'll leave you to have a discussion while I get the wine ready." With that, she twirled on her heel. Her robe swirling around her made the movement seem like a grand gesture. She waited impatiently in the adjacent room, straining to hear the conversation through the door. The whole plan teetered on the edge of a precipice. She heard plenty of questions and very few relevant answers filtering through the cracks in the old door. She crossed her fingers and squeezed her eyes shut. They fluttered open, and she swiftly moved away from the door when she heard faint footsteps on the other side. After a gentle tap, the door swung open. Elaine stood there, her expression unreadable.

The hairs on the back of Felicity's neck stood up in anticipation. "Well?" she asked, finally unable to bear the suspense any longer.

"We've managed to talk her around."

Felicity punched the air with a clenched fist. That's all the jubilation she showed, despite wanting to run around the room with joy, stark naked. "Okay, and she's going to stick with us, see it through to the end? Or will she cause more upset and want to back out further down the line, do you think?"

"I wouldn't like to say what will happen in the future. The other girls were keen to point out the error in her ways. We'll just have to be happy with that right now."

"I suppose so. Okay, I'll be with you in a moment." Felicity dismissed Elaine and walked across the room to the boxes of wine in the corner. She set out the plastic glasses, filling each one with the merlot, and carried the tray back into the other room. The group smiled hesitantly until a smile lit her own face. "Grab a glass, girls. Our mission is about to begin in earnest."

Dara was the last to retrieve her glass, still avoiding Felicity's gaze. She offered the woman the hand of peace. Dara shook it, and slowly, her eyes locked with Felicity's. "We can do this, Dara. Stay strong and positive throughout, my love."

Dara half-smiled and took a sip of wine from her glass. "I'll try. I can't promise more than that."

"Then I can't ask for more. Are you willing to proceed in the order suggested, that Jordan should be next?"

Dara's slim shoulders lifted to touch her ears. "I suppose so. Do I have to be here while he's being tortured?"

"That's the idea, hon. We need to make him feel sorry for what he's done to you. It wouldn't have the same effect if you weren't there to see him suffer, would it?"

Another shrug and the wisp of a smile gave Felicity her answer.

"Okay, let me have your attention, ladies."

The room fell silent.

"Thank you. Dara, you said that Jordan works in the city but also has an office near home. Is that right?"

"Yes, he spends most of the working week at the office not far from his house. He only pops into London when there's a major board meeting going on."

"That's great to know. I want to pick him up tomorrow evening. I bet he knocks off work bang on time, yes?"

"He does. He always states that the firm gets enough blood, sweat, and tears out of him in eight hours. Why should he work any longer than that? He leaves at six on the dot every night, rain or shine."

The more she heard about the man, the more Felicity disliked him. She'd never even heard of an accountant living and working by the clock. Yes, she was looking forward to meeting and dealing with Jordan. "Then I think we should make arrangements for a group of us to meet at five tomorrow. We can all pile into my car and wait for him to leave his place of business at six. We'll pounce on him like we did Don."

"No. You can't do that. Look how that ended," Dara argued.

"This will be different, I can assure you. You've intimated in the past that he has a roving eye where the ladies are concerned."

Dara nodded reluctantly.

"Well, that's going to be to our advantage, isn't it, ladies?"

The women raised their glasses and cheered.

"We have enough beauties around here to tempt him. We'll take a decoy car. Who's willing to act as bait?"

The room fell quiet again, until Kaz, a beautiful brunette, cleared her throat and put her hand in the air.

"Kaz, I think you'll do just fine. We'll run through the details later. Do you have a problem with scheduling this for tomorrow evening?"

"Not in the least. I'll drop the kids off at their grandmother's house for tea and come here. It's not far from my mother's house anyway."

"Good, good. Maybe those of you with children should make similar arrangements? We could be looking at a late night tomorrow if things go according to plan."

"How late?" Dara asked. "You will set Jordan free that evening, won't you?"

"I can't promise that, Dara. It really depends on how Jordan behaves himself. It would be better if you made provisions for your kids to stay overnight somewhere just in case the evening lengthens into an all-nighter."

Dara's horrified expression returned. However, Felicity chose to ignore it this time for fear they'd end up going in circles if she acknowledged it. Another hour of drinking and small talk passed, then they got down to the nitty-gritty of cementing their strategy. Once that had been thrashed out, the group drifted away, leaving Felicity to ensure everything was ready for the new arrival the following evening.

She went into the cellar, to the room where the punishment would take place, away from the sanctity of the altar and the goodness that entailed, into the depths of despair where their victims were sure to crap themselves once the torture had commenced. Behind the black curtain, she checked the stocks, which the others were unaware of. When she had sanctioned the builder to erect the articles in the cellar, he had smiled broadly, and she knew instantly what the sick bastard had been thinking before he even opened his smutty mouth.

"Into a bit of S&M, are you, love? Give me a call if you need a new volunteer."

She had laughed loudly at the suggestion but quickly found herself playing along because it would be the perfect ruse to avoid suspicion if the stocks were ever found. "Damn, and there I was, thinking I was being discreet. You won't say anything, will you?" Then she had shocked the man by leaning in and whispering, "My other half loves it. We take it in turns. She prefers being chained up more than I do, though, fancy that."

The fat builder's eyes almost dropped out of their sockets. "She? So you're a lesbo, then. Er… I mean a lesbian."

"Oh, yes. A woman has specific needs only other women recognise and can fulfil."

"You're kidding. Listen, love, you've been with the wrong type of blokes. Spend a night with me, and I'll show you what you've been missing out on all these years. Hey, you can bring your partner, too. I've never had a threesome before, but I'm definitely up for that."

Felicity's smile remained firmly in place. Inside she cringed and cursed herself for putting such thoughts into the man's head. He was gross beyond words, and until he'd completed the job, she'd kept her distance from him.

Men, all they ever think about is sex. Well, she intended putting a stop to that, starting with this Jordan fella. He had made Dara's life hell, cheating on her with every woman willing to smile his way during their marriage, and pitifully, Dara had just accepted it as the norm. She checked the locks on the shackles then pulled the curtain across to disguise the equipment. She went home, and sleep eventually came that night, early morning actually, as one by one, the pieces of her cunning plan slotted into place.

CHAPTER FOUR

Lorne checked on Onyx and her pups first thing the next day. It was only six thirty, but the dogs' plight had filled her mind all night when sleep evaded her. If she had been alone, she would have checked on the dog at two or three in the morning to put her mind at ease, but she didn't want to wake Tony. Onyx raised her head when Lorne entered the kennel. Crouching beside the sorrowful pooch, she stroked her. The dog's tail twitched and soon fell into a regular rhythm, thrashing against Lorne's leg.

"Hello, gorgeous. Feeling a little better, are we?" She shuffled closer and pulled the blanket covering the cold kennel floor into a bunch under her backside, positioning herself next to the dog. Two of the pups stirred and latched onto their mother's teats, wanting their breakfast before the others woke up. Onyx stretched a little so that her head brushed Lorne's lap. She touched the dog's head and slowly ran her hand down her body, noting that the dog's skin felt cooler to the touch beneath the T-shirt. There was no denying though that even if the medication was beginning to take effect, the poor dog still had a very long way to go before she regained her fur. Not for the first time, Lorne cursed the person who had given this dog such a terrible start in life, and she silently wished the same fate would descend on that human in the near future. Of course, there was little chance of anything as satisfying as that truly happening.

Lost in angry thoughts, she neglected to feel the dog licking the back of her hand, which had come to a stop on the dog's side. Lorne smiled at the first sign of trust Onyx had shown toward a human after being let down so badly. She spent another peaceful ten minutes with the dog then headed back into the house to prepare breakfast. She was in the mood for the works.

A noisy yawn preceded her husband into the kitchen. "Do I smell bacon?" He slid his arms around her waist and rested his head on her back.

"You do. I thought I'd surprise you and Charlie, for a change. Did I keep you awake last night? I hardly slept."

"No. I felt you move a few times, but I was exhausted and fell back to sleep fairly quickly. Was Onyx on your mind during the night?"

She flicked the bacon and rotated the sausages in the frying pan then turned in his arms to face him. As they kissed, Lorne felt the stresses of Onyx's situation drift away. "Yeah, I think I'm finally getting somewhere with her. I've been out there for a while, and she reacted to my touch by licking my hand. I think the medication is doing the trick. Her skin feels cooler. Let's hope the infected skin and scabs heal quickly. I sense her being around for a good few months yet."

"I'd rather hang on to her for a while anyway. Let's make her road to recovery a special one, eh? I'll get Charlie to spend a little time with her every day, walking her in the exercise pen without the pups for a few minutes every afternoon. How's that?"

"Sounds just what she needs to get back on her feet again. What if she was from one of those awful puppy mills?"

Tony shook his head. "I doubt it. Those places are all about the money. If that was the case, the unscrupulous owner would have kept the puppies and dumped her." He motioned toward the pan. "Is that nearly ready?"

Lorne nodded. "Yes, can you give Charlie a shout for me?"

The family shared their first breakfast in a long while, then Lorne showered and set off for work, wondering what the day would bring for Don Alder's case.

Katy and AJ were sharing a joke at his desk when Lorne pushed through the incident room door.

"Morning, both." She smiled and winked at them.

Katy's eyes rolled up to the ceiling. "Good morning, Lorne. How's the pup doing?"

Lorne sat down at her desk and booted up her computer. "She seems a little more trusting today. I'm hoping that's a sign that she's feeling a little better. Her skin isn't so inflamed, so that's a blessing, I suppose. What's on the agenda today, boss?"

"That's what AJ and I were discussing when you came in."

Lorne raised a quizzical eyebrow and swallowed the sarcastic comment teetering on her lips. "And?"

"And we think we've managed to trace the sister and the wife, the last known address we have for them anyway. We'll head out this morning and take a gander, all right?"

"Oh, how did that come about? The landlord is still away on holiday, isn't he?"

Katy left AJ's desk and walked towards her office. "It's called detective work, detective. You wanna try it sometime?" she fired over her shoulder before she closed the door.

Lorne jabbed a thumb in Katy's direction. "Get her. Are you going to let me in on your secret, AJ?"

"I searched a few databases and stumbled across the answers, Lorne. There's no telling if the information is what we're looking for yet. But it might well lead onto some valuable info."

"You're the man for obtaining such info, so well done, you. I just need to make a quick call, and I'll be with you." Lorne tapped a few keys of the computer then placed a call. "Hello, I wonder if you can help me. I run a rescue centre for abandoned dogs and wondered if you would be interested in running a story about us?"

"That sounds interesting. Can I have your name, and I'll get one of our programme directors to give you a call back."

"Thank you. It's Lorne Warner. I'll give you my mobile number, if that's okay? I'll probably be out most of the day—I usually am."

"I thought you said you run a rescue centre. You mean you're constantly rounding dogs up to take in?" The young woman waited for clarification.

Lorne laughed. "No, I'm also a detective sergeant in the Met."

"Cool. So you're a glutton for punishment and a workaholic, to boot?"

"I have a supportive family running the rescue centre. Phew, that should clear that up. The reason I'm ringing is because I've just taken in a very sorry-looking dog, covered in mange. I'm desperate to get the word out about her. You know, maybe someone will be able to identify her and tell us who the owner is so that we can prosecute them. But the main reason I'm eager for some exposure is to try to find a loving forever home for her and her pups."

"Pups?"

"She has four, all adorable and, thankfully, mange free."

"Bless, what a terrible shame. Let's see what we can do. Hold the line please."

Lorne tapped her pen on the desk while she listened to music on the line until the lady returned.

"Okay, we're going to squeeze you in on our usual pet slot. Is that all right? The vet could give a few pointers on how to detect if your dog has mange and what to do in the event to combat the condition. How does that sound?"

"Bloody brilliant. I never dreamed I'd get this kind of response from you. I'm so grateful. When?"

"Can I make the arrangements and get back to you later today?"

"Yes, of course. Sorry, I didn't get your name?"

"It's Tara. I'm an animal lover, too, Lorne, and I'd just like to thank you for saving at least a few of the dogs out there who've been abandoned. People like you should be recognised more in the Queen's birthday honour list."

Lorne's cheeks flared up. "Nonsense, I don't do it for the recognition. I do it for the sake of the dogs. No dog deserves to be treated like that. Thanks again, Tara. Speak to you later. I really appreciate your help."

"No probs. Speak soon."

"That sounded promising, Lorne," AJ said, glancing up from his paperwork.

"Maybe I caught her on a good day. I'll just let Katy know. Talking of which…" She lowered her voice and called over, "Any news in that department?"

AJ shook his head and checked to see if the coast was clear before he replied, "Not sure, really. I think she's having problems with her folks. Mind you, there's always some form of trouble in the way. Maybe we're just not meant to be together."

Lorne left her desk and crossed the room towards him. "Hey, don't be so defeatist. If ever a couple belonged together, it's you two. Hang in there, sweetheart. If it's meant to be, nothing will stand in the way of true love."

As if on cue, Katy's office door opened, and she joined them. "Should my ears be burning?"

"Nope. I was just telling AJ that I've managed to grab a spot on the local TV station."

Katy frowned. "What? To do with the case?"

"No. To do with Onyx, the doggy we found. They're going to feature her in the regular pet slot. I call that a result, don't you?"

"I should say. Okay, now you've sorted out your personal business on police time, what say we get back to trying to solve the crime in hand?"

"Where would you like to start?" Lorne asked as the rest of the team noisily marched into the room.

Katy's eyes shot up to the clock on the wall. "Only just, people. Two minutes to nine is cutting it a bit fine."

"Yes, boss," Karen, Graham, and Stephen all said in unison, looking a little sheepish.

"AJ, while Lorne and I are out, tracking down and questioning Alder's relatives, can you get the rest of the team organised? Finish up last week's cases and delve deeper into Alder's past maybe. There must have been some kind of motive for the attack, even if it's the unlikely scenario that he bumped into a prostitute on the street." She clicked her fingers. "See if he had any previous convictions for curb crawling, anything of that ilk. We need to find something in case Lorne and I draw a blank while we're out."

"Okeydokey. I'll get on it now. Leave this rabble for me to sort out."

"Bloody cheek," Karen, the young detective constable complained light-heartedly.

Katy smiled and pointed at AJ. "He's the boss when we're not around. Any complaints land on *his* desk, not mine. See you later."

Lorne and Katy left the station and drove to the first address AJ had given them. The flat was about a five-minute walk from Alder's flat. "Here we are, number six."

"Let's see if his sister is in. We might be lucky at this time of day, unless she's an office cleaner or something similar, just on her way home from work." Lorne eyed the peeling paint of the windows and doors.

"Only one way to find out." Katy strode up the narrow path and knocked on the front door of what looked like a maisonette, with Lorne bringing up the rear.

A woman in her mid-to-late fifties opened the door with a scowl etched into her wrinkled face. "Yes?"

"Alice Alder?"

"Who wants to know?"

Katy pulled out her ID. "Detective Inspector Katy Foster of the Met. Are you Alice Alder?"

"Yes." A nervous pitch developed in her tone. "What do you want?"

"It's about your brother Don."

"Have you arrested him?"

"What makes you think that? Should we be arresting him, Ms. Alder?"

"No… what other reason would there be for you to visit me out of the blue like this?" She gasped then covered her mouth with her hand.

"I'm so sorry, but your brother was found dead outside the Sloane Hospital yesterday. We've been trying to trace you ever since."

The colour drained from the woman's face, then she turned and headed back into the flat. Lorne and Katy shrugged at each other and followed her up the hallway and into the lounge. The first thing Ms. Alder did was reach for a cigarette. She stood in the bay window, looking out at life still going on outside, seemingly lost in a world of her own.

Katy cleared her throat. "I know it must be a shock to hear the news, Ms. Alder, but if there is anything you can tell us that will help us catch your brother's killer, it would help."

Slowly with a furrowed brow, the woman stared at Katy. "Killer? He didn't die of natural causes?"

"No, I'm sorry. Although I'm led to believe by the pathologist that your brother suffered a heart attack around the time of the attack, our first impressions that he'd died a natural death were quickly discounted. We found blood at the scene. During the post mortem, it was determined that your brother had received a blow to his leg, we think from a stiletto."

"What? A woman did this?" Ms. Alder sat down heavily on the patched-up sofa.

"At this point, that would be our assumption. But there's always the idea that the killer might be male and that the stiletto was used to put us off the scent. That sort of thing wouldn't be unheard of in crimes such as this, where no other clues are found at the scene."

"I see."

"I have to ask—your brother was married until recently, wasn't he?" Katy said.

Lorne took out her notebook, ready to jot down information.

"He was, to Julie. To be honest, I'm still not sure what went wrong with their marriage for it to end so abruptly. One month, we were all talking about going away together for Christmas, and the next, Don told me they were getting a divorce."

Lorne filled the momentary silence by asking, "Did they say on what grounds?"

"Not really. As far as I was concerned, they had a loving relationship. What do I know? Maybe they just put on a show when I was around. If they were that happy, they wouldn't have divorced, would they?"

"Can you tell us how long they were married?" Katy asked.

"Around fifteen years, I think."

"And to you, everything was fine between Don and Julie?"

The woman looked perplexed. "Yes, I've just said." She took another puff of her cigarette and thought the question over some more then added with a gasp, "My God, you don't think Julie had anything to do with this?"

"Well, we can't rule her out, especially after what the neighbour told us this morning."

Ms. Alder's head inclined. "What was that?"

"That Don and Julie were prone to having a lot of arguments. Are you telling me that you're unaware of that?"

"They had disagreements, often. I wouldn't really call them arguments, though."

"Maybe they kept that side of things under wraps from you, too. Can you tell me where we can find this Julie Alder?" Katy asked with a smile.

"I'm not really sure. Let me check in my address book, see if I have the new address. I can't think straight right now." Ms. Alder left the room and returned with her handbag. She extracted a small pocket diary and turned to the address book section. "I'm sorry, no. I don't even have a telephone number I can give you. How lax of me."

"Would you say you used to be good friends?"

"Yes, that's why I'm surprised I haven't jotted down her new address. I was so sure I had it when we last met."

"When did you see your ex-sister-in-law last?"

"Let me think... around a month ago, I believe."

"This is so frustrating," Katy said.

Lorne shot her a glance, praying that her partner would keep calm.

"Are you sure you didn't pick up anything that might give us a clue as to where she's calling home now?" Katy asked.

"No, I'm so sorry. No one is more upset about that than I am, I assure you. Maybe it was intentional on her part. You know, in case I passed the information on to Don. Not that I would have if she hadn't wanted me to. Now he's gone, and..."

Katy huffed out a sigh. "And the only possible lead we have could be living in Timbuktu for all we know."

"Oh no, I don't think she would have gone that far," Ms. Alder quickly shot back, soon realising her mistake. "Sorry, that was dumb of me. She's definitely still in the area. Of that much, I'm certain."

Lorne coughed quietly to gain Katy's attention. "Ms. Alder, perhaps you can tell us what bank she uses?"

"Good idea," Katy praised her partner.

"Not so good, really. She didn't believe in banks. You can't trust them, she used to say. I'm inclined to agree with her after the banking debacles we've witnessed in recent times."

"Another dead end. We're getting nowhere fast today," Katy complained.

"I'm sorry," the woman repeated. "Can I see my brother?"

"Of course. My partner can ring the mortuary and arrange a visit. Will you do that, Lorne? While I keep asking Ms. Alder some questions, something might come to mind that will help us."

"Of course. I'll be right back." Lorne left the room to ring Patti. "Hi, it's Lorne. We're at the victim's sister's house. She'd like to visit her brother ASAP."

"Tell her she can come in this afternoon between three and four, Lorne. How are things going with the case? Or shouldn't I ask?"

"Nope, you shouldn't. All we've found out so far is that their marriage broke up, and the neighbour residing in the flat above Mr. Alder said they used to have a lot of lover's tiffs. Nothing else has come to light yet. What about you?"

"Nothing noteworthy as yet. An injury to the head I missed on the initial examination."

"Oh? Maybe the victim was knocked out and then stamped on with the heel while he lay on the ground?"

"Maybe, Lorne. We could speculate about that all day and not really come up with the correct answer. Anyway, I've got to fly. Talk soon."

"Thanks, Patti." Lorne went back into the lounge to relay the pathologist's message regarding the visiting times. "Between three and four this afternoon."

"Thank you, I'll be there. I really don't think there is anything else I can tell you about Julie. She doesn't work because she was made redundant about a year ago."

Lorne took out her notebook again. "From where?"

"Let me see… there's a small library in Gravesend." Ms. Alder waved a hand at them and shook her head. "Silly me, she was made redundant because they closed down."

"Great." Lorne tutted.

"Oh, well, we'll leave you now, Ms. Alder. If you remember anything, please give us a call. Here's my card." Katy handed the card to the woman then made her way to the front door.

"I will. Thank you for coming to tell me about my brother. I really appreciate it." Her voice shook as though she would break down in tears once she saw them off the property.

"I hope we'll have some good news for you soon. Bye for now."

Lorne nodded at the woman as she brushed past her in the hallway. "Goodbye. My condolences again."

The door closed behind them. Both detectives let out a frustrated sigh once they returned to the car.

Katy slapped the steering wheel. "What are the odds on the sister-in-law vanishing into thin air like that? If I didn't know any better, I'd say this was a planned attack and she's spent months setting it up, going so far as to cover her tracks since the day she left the marital home."

"It certainly looks that way to me. The question is, how do we either link her to the crime or find out where she's hiding?" Just as she finished speaking, Lorne's mobile rang. "Hello?"

"Lorne, it's Tara at the TV station."

"Hi, Tara. I hope you have some good news for me. I could sure do with some."

"Sorry you're having a bad day. Hopefully this will cheer you up. Can you bring the dog in tomorrow?"

"Gosh, that soon? What time?"

"I've made special arrangements, mindful of your career, for the interview to be filmed around seven in the evening. How does that sound to you?"

She glanced sideways and winked at Katy. "Sounds great. I'll have a word with my boss, see if I can go home earlier than normal. Shall I just report to reception when I arrive?"

"Yes, I'll let them know you've got an interview arranged. I should be around, so I'll see you then, Lorne."

"Thanks, Tara." She disconnected the call. "Can I leave a little early tomorrow? I have to go home and get back into London by seven. That will be difficult if I finish work around six, like normal."

"I'm sure we can come to some arrangement. Right, where do we go from here?" Katy said.

"Back to the station, see if the gang has managed to dig anything else up."

"I doubt it, but there's nothing else we can do out here."

Katy drove back to the station while Lorne rang home to tell Tony and Charlie the good news.

"Charlie, how is Onyx?"

"Hi, Mum. She's fine, learning to trust a bit more every time I go in the kennel to see her. Shall I bathe her again today? I think it's helping."

"Yep, I thought the vet said she had to be bathed every day? I have exciting news for you."

"Yeah, he did. Go on, surprise me," Charlie said, exasperation evident in her teenage voice.

"Onyx is booked in for an interview with the local TV station tomorrow."

"Mum, you can't do that to the poor dog, parade her on screen looking like that."

"She'll be covered up with my T-shirt, love. It'll be good to show the general public what the poor thing is going through."

Charlie let out a heavy sigh. "I suppose you're right. I'm looking at this from her point of view, though. She's just learning to trust us, and now you want to whisk her out of her safe surroundings into a manic arena."

"Overstating the point, as usual, dearest child of mine. I understand your misgivings, but the sooner we do this interview, the quicker we're likely to get the person who treated her so badly banged up. Yes?"

"Yeees! Buuut!"

"I'm on the way back to the station now. Will you pass the message on to Tony for me please?"

"Okay, going now. Laters."

Lorne hung up. "I swear, she gets worse every day. She's definitely starting to see the world and circumstances through fresh eyes."

"And that's a bad thing?"

"No, I'm not saying that. Sometimes she can be a handful to contain, though. Her enthusiasm for the dogs and her protective nature are bound to get her in trouble one of these days. I never dreamed she would take on the role with such enthusiasm."

"She has her mother's determination and compassion running through her. Let's put it this way—I never had any doubts about her making the rescue centre a success. Does Tony actually have any input into that place now?"

"Thinking about it, you're right—I don't really think he has. He's Charlie's odd-job man most of the time. Not sure I can see any other ex-MI6 officer being happy taking orders from a stroppy teenager, can you?"

They both laughed riotously at the thought.

CHAPTER FIVE

Felicity appeared to be watching the clock all afternoon, until finally, five o'clock struck on the grandfather clock in the hallway. *Time to move into position.* "Let's go, girls. Get this task over with. We'll be right back," she announced to the girls who had been nominated to remain at the cottage.

The two cars drove out to the retail park on the outskirts of the town and parked. Kaz joined Mags, Elaine, Sally, and Felicity in the other car, and they ran through the plan one final time as they waited for six o'clock to come around. At five forty-five, aware of what she needed to do to entice Jordan, Kaz hopped back into her car. Felicity observed her friend closely, fearing that she would start her engine and leave the scene before they had the chance to grab their next victim.

The time dragged by, then at two minutes to six, Jordan came out the rear of the building. Using Dara's photograph of her ex, the women recognised him right away. And there was no mistaking his arrogance, either, from the way he walked to the way he dressed. There was no confusion about the quality of his suit.

Felicity could see Kaz begin to get fidgety in her seat. She crossed her fingers, willing her friend not to back out.

"Come on, Kaz. Another few steps, and he'll be within your grasp."

"She looks nervous," Mags said. "Do you think she'll drive off?"

"I'm hoping not. I agree—she does seem exceedingly anxious. Ah, there it is, the devastating smile she always puts into place when she wants something."

"She's getting out now." Elaine sat forward on the edge of the backseat. "Get him, Kaz."

Each of the women in the car took a sharp breath when Kaz opened the car door and stepped elegantly from the vehicle. She tugged the hem down on her mid-thigh skirt and smiled at the man approaching her. Felicity pushed the button to lower the car window, but the pair were too far away for her to hear the exchange. Their body language was obvious enough, though. Kaz led Jordan around the front of the vehicle and opened the bonnet of her car. Jordan peered underneath, trying to help the faux damsel in distress. Kaz appeared at the side of the car and waved her arm, encouraging them to get a move on.

"Right, that's our cue to get involved, girls. Are you ready?"

A mumbled reply came from each of the women, and they all left the car. The four of them tiptoed across the car park and stopped at the rear of the vehicle, awaiting further instructions from Kaz. Her signal came soon after, in the form of another hand gesture. This time, Felicity got the impression Kaz was eager to put the situation to bed.

Felicity pointed for Mags and Sally to take the route down one side of the car while she and Elaine went down the other. Jordan was talking smutty to his captive audience. Her stomach constricted and churned the more she heard the sickliness of his words. Shuddering away her disgust, she took a long breath to calm herself, knowing that there would be no point attacking the man if she was full of rage.

Giving the thumbs-up to Mags and Sally, they moved into position in unison.

"Hi, Kaz, who's your friend?"

The smile broadened on Jordan's face; to be surrounded by beautiful women was a man's ultimate dream, wasn't it? Felicity's plan had worked, at least the initial signs were proving to be good. Jordan was definitely living up to his notorious reputation; she couldn't foresee any problems with successfully slotting the next part of their scheme into action.

"I'm not sure, Kaz replied, "I forgot to get your name, what is it?"

"David," he replied with a smirk.

"What?" Felicity shouted, stupefied.

"David Calleja. And your names are? I prefer to know who I am speaking to."

"It doesn't matter what our names are. Yours is definitely David and not Jordan?"

The man's head tipped back when he laughed. "So you know my twin brother."

Behind them a man's voice boomed out. "Did I hear my name mentioned? Hello, ladies. Do I know you?"

Shit, damn and blast! Why hadn't Dara warned us he had a twin who worked at the same frim? Bugger, what do we do now?

Thinking on her feet, Felicity said, "No. We're friends of Dara. She told us that you like to party and we wondered if you'd be up for a special celebration we have planned for this evening."

Jordan pointed to his chest. "Just me? Or would it be all right if my brother joined us?" Jordan's eyebrows wiggled. He might have thought the movement was seductive, but Felicity had to force back the rising bile. The man was gross, so full of crap that if he exploded, it would cover the Sahara Desert twice over.

"That's up to David. Have you got anything special planned tonight?" Felicity asked with a broad smile.

"No, as it happens, I don't have anything on this evening. Just a minute…"

Uh oh, I think he's the brighter of the two men. I know what's coming next.

David continued to look perplexed and rubbed his chin between his forefinger and thumb. "I don't understand why you would invite Jordan to a party. It's not like he and Dara parted on good terms, is it?"

She waved a hand in front of her. "We're on the lookout for men who enjoy a good time with the ladies. We fell out with Dara a long time ago. The thing is, when I was planning this party, I remember her mentioning that Jordan used to be the life and soul of every party they threw. Some of the men we had lined up for this evening's *entertainment* had to drop out at the last minute." She winked at both men. "There's always room for two handsome guys like you to join us. Eh, girls?"

"Oh, yes." Mags ran a hand slowly down the length of Jordan's arm. His smile stretched farther, if that were at all possible.

Jordan shook his head light-heartedly at his brother. "Come on, bro. I won't tell your missus."

That one comment summed up the despicable man. Felicity totted up all the torture techniques she had lined up for the man and doubled them in an instant.

David hesitated for several seconds. Kaz didn't disappoint—she placed her hands on his shoulders and whispered something in his ear, bringing an unexpected flush to his cheeks.

He nodded. "All right. I'll come, on one proviso."

"Which is?" Kaz fluttered her eyelashes at him.

"That you and I spend some time together away from this lot."

Kaz giggled. "I think that can be arranged, sweetie. The pleasure will be all mine, in fact."

Jordan rubbed his hands together in glee. "Good job, bro. Right, now that's sorted, where's the part-tee?"

Felicity's excitement started to mount again once that certain obstacle had been overcome. "We'll go in our cars. We can drop you back here either later on or tomorrow. How does that sound?"

"Sounds good to me. I like the idea of an all-nighter. Don't you, bro?" Jordan agreed, sounding keen.

"Okay by me," David said, giving Kaz a toothy smile.

"Right, Kaz and Mags, why don't you take David with you? And Jordan can come in my car with Elaine and Sally. You can keep the girls company in the back while I drive," Felicity said, winking at Jordan.

The group split up. As they walked back to Felicity's car, Jordan threw an arm around the two ladies accompanying him.

He's just too full of himself, that one.

When the group arrived at the darkened cottage, the women teasingly showed the two men into the house.

"Hey, put some lights on?" Jordan complained.

"No, it's more atmospheric like this. Girls, hold our guests' hands, and we'll show them where the party is. The other girls should have completed the preparations by now."

"You mean there are more of you?" David asked.

Kaz sniggered. "Yes, but you're all mine. You wouldn't be able to handle anyone else."

They wound their way through the cottage, along the familiar route the women knew by heart, down the stairs to the cellar.

Felicity called out, "We're here girls. Is everything set up?"

Silence filled the damp, musty room, then a little voice said, "We're ready and waiting, Oh Merciful One."

Felicity cringed, hoping that the strange label wouldn't raise their guests' suspicions. She heard the cellar door close at the top of the stairs after the final person had passed through the doorway.

Only a few more steps, and everyone would be on level ground, where the men would be easier to subdue.

"Go!" she shouted. Within seconds, the room started to glow as numerous candles were lit.

"Ooo... I like this," Jordan uttered. "It's nice having a little intimacy with a lady or two."

There will be plenty of intimacy. Don't you worry about that, my dear friend.

As the room grew lighter, the wider Jordan's grin spread. His brother, on the other hand, looked more and more perplexed. Felicity recognised the distrust pooling in his eyes and reached out to try to put him at ease. Her expectations of how the evening would pan out had shifted with his inclusion. The last thing she wanted was for everything to go awry.

"David, why don't you make yourself comfortable over there with Kaz?" She pointed at a couple of cushioned chairs off to one side of the room. "And you, Jordan, can stay here with us."

"Yeah, go on, bro. Go have yourself a good time with Kaz. It looks like I'm going to have my hands full here for a while, if you get my drift."

Out of the corner of her eye, Felicity noticed the curtain twitch. Her heart sank when she realised Dara was hiding behind it. *Stay there. Stay out of sight, at least for now.* But she had a feeling that Dara was about to do just the opposite. She needed to act fast, before Jordan's ex gave away the game.

"Why don't we organise some drinks and then start the party games. Mags, can you sort out the music? I put a variety of albums over there by the tape machine."

"My pleasure. Hot and raunchy or slow and deliberate?"

"Let's go with hot and raunchy and see where that leads us, hey, Jordan?"

His eyes widened to their fullest, and he growled like an animal in heat. "Oh, yes, hot and raunchy sounds delicious to me."

She suspected her warm smile hid her repulsion well. She guided Jordan to the seats on the opposite side of the room then went in search of the promised drinks. A few women were already in the back room, filling the glasses with red wine.

"Okay, I need you to pass the message around while I help keep the men distracted. We're going to play with them for a while, lead them into believing we have the intention of sleeping with them later. Once their defences drop—it shouldn't take long in Jordan's case—then we pounce."

Dara quietly joined her. "How could you?"

"What, Dara? We haven't done anything yet."

"You know what I mean. You're not stupid. His brother, David—how could you get him involved in all of this? He's married to a wonderful woman. I wouldn't feel right about hurting him."

"Well, maybe he should have considered his *wonderful* wife before he accompanied his brother on this little outing. Men always show their true colours when the chips are down, Dara. It's very rare they think with their heads instead of their dicks when a little loving is on offer."

Dara sank back against the wall, and her chin fell onto her chest. "I've changed my mind," she mumbled sullenly.

"What? It's far too late for that now. They're here. They've seen our hideout—we can't let them go now." She corrected herself quickly, knowing that the men would never see daylight again if everything went according to her plan. "Not yet."

Dara raised her head, and with narrowed eyes, she asked, "You are going to let them go, though, aren't you, Felicity?"

She waved off the woman's concern. "Eventually, yes. Let's have some fun with them first, girl. Look, if you feel uncomfortable about seeing this, then go home. I'd be very disappointed if you chose that option, however. Stay in here, out of sight, for the next hour or so and then make your appearance when things start to heat up. I want him to see that you are no longer scared of him. Don't you want that, too, hon?"

Dara inhaled and let the breath out almost immediately. "Maybe. Oh, I just don't know anymore. Now the time has arrived, I'm having second thoughts about the situation. Please reconsider until I can figure things out in here." She prodded at her temple.

Felicity shook her head. "I've already told you that things are going ahead as scheduled. It would be a wasted opportunity if we backed out now. The option wouldn't arise again in the future, love. Take my word on that. Do as I say—stay in here for the time being, all right?"

Reluctantly, Dara crossed the room, picked up a glass of wine, and dropped onto a tiny wooden stool in the corner, the only form of seating in the room. "Give me a shout when you're ready. And, Felicity, please be gentle with him. I couldn't live with the guilt of seeing him hurt."

"You worry too much. We'll see you soon." Felicity motioned for the other girls to bring the drinks and to join the rest of the women looking after their two guests. "Here we are. I hope you like red wine, boys?"

Jordan snatched the glass out of her hand and downed the drink in two large gulps. "Yep, I need a top up. When does the real entertainment begin? That's what I'd like to know." He ran his tongue suggestively around his plump lips.

"Real entertainment? Well that only happens to men who behave and learn to control themselves, Jordan. You could learn a thing or two from your brother's behaviour."

"Ha! He's always been the quiet one in the family. The most excitement he's had in his life is when he caught a ten-pound trout on a fishing holiday in France." He laughed at his own joke.

Felicity's gaze drifted over to David. She could tell that underneath his cool exterior, there was an angry man wanting to punch his brother's lights out for the public humiliation he was subjecting him to.

The music started up and combatted the tension between the men. The 1980s disco tunes appeared to go down well, and before long, everyone was up on their feet moving. Some were even gyrating and twerking to the beat. Jordan was well on his way to inebriation, which Felicity hoped would make their job much easier when the time came to place him in the stocks. Her brain had been working overtime and had come up with several ideas on how to get him into the contraption. She'd finally settled on the idea that he would be up for a game where kinky sex was on offer. After a few more drinks, he would be a willing participant—of that, she was confident.

Two more glasses of wine, and even David had loosened the black tie around his neck and seemed to be enjoying himself. His brown eyes sparkled with what looked like devilment, and his arm had become permanently fixed around Kaz's shoulder. The temptress gave Felicity the impression she would be happy to put up with his mauling, aware of how the evening would end for the brothers.

It was time to escalate things and aim for the end game. Felicity tugged Jordan's shirt out of his suit trousers and started unbuttoning it, while sashaying her hips. She heard him gulp and knew he was under her spell. Halfway through undoing the buttons, she placed a hand around his tie and swivelled, pulling his tie over her shoulder then leading him toward the stocks. Felicity glanced sideways to see

Kaz mirroring her movements, bringing David along, as well. Her heart rate tripled, and she cast aside the fears suddenly filling her mind with scenarios of what could go wrong.

One of the girls changed the music to something with a conga beat, and everyone joined in the fun. The men were oblivious to what was going on. Finally, Felicity came to a halt in front of one set of stocks, and Kaz slipped past her to deposit David by the other set.

"Let's make things a little more interesting, shall we, boys?" She glanced at Kaz and winked.

"Just tell us what to do." Jordan's eagerness brought her attention back to him.

"Take a seat. You too, David."

The two men plonked down on the cushioned bench.

Felicity dropped to her knees in front of Jordan, and Kaz did the same with his brother.

"Give me your hands and feet." Felicity removed Jordan's shoes and socks and put the shackles around his ankles. The sound of the women observers standing behind her urged her to finish the task quickly before they gave the game away. She heard Kaz removing David's shoes, following her movements to the letter.

Snap, snap, snap, and *snap.* Four shackles snapped into place around two ankles and two wrists. Jordan laughed and looked over as Kaz completed the same action with David. Felicity and Kaz stood up and stepped back a foot or so then high-fived each other.

"Right. I hate to repeat myself, but this is where the true games begin." Felicity raised her voice. "You can come out now."

Dara entered the room with her head bowed low.

Colour rose from Jordan's neck and flooded his cheeks. His head shook in disbelief. "You! What are you doing here?"

Dara came to a standstill alongside Felicity, within inches of Jordan's feet. "I'm sorry, Jordan. Please forgive me?"

"Forgive you? For what?" His brow twisted into a deep crease.

"That's enough, Dara."

"But I need to hear that he forgives me, Felicity."

"I don't understand. Why should I forgive you? What's going on here?" Jordan yanked and twisted his constraints, to no avail.

"Oh no!" David groaned.

Kaz struck him across the top of the head with her open hand. "Hush now. The better you behave, the less punishment you'll receive."

"I knew it. What sort of crap have you got us caught up in now, brother?" David asked, shifting uncomfortably, making his chains jangle noisily.

"Shut up. I came to your rescue, remember? You're to blame for this."

"No. I think you'll find this is about retribution for all the pain and anguish you put Dara through during your farce of a marriage," David countered, living up to Felicity's assumption that he was the brainier of the two men.

She made a note to be gentle with the man compared to what she had in store for Jordan.

"What? Our marriage wasn't a farce, not until the end. She loved me unconditionally, and I loved her in return. Didn't I, Dara?"

"Yes, dear," Dara said, her head still lowered.

"Don't do it, Dara. Don't let him continue to manipulate you. Yes, David, you're totally correct in your assumption as to why you gentlemen are here with us tonight. It's all about retribution, Jordan. David, I want to say from the outset, that I apologise for your involvement in this. We didn't know Jordan had a brother, let alone a twin, who worked at the same firm. Your role in this is noted, and we'll be kinder to you as a consequence. You have my word on that."

David inclined his head. "Thank you. If you'll consider letting me go, I promise that I won't go to the police. My brother has been walking a tightrope for years. Something like this was bound to happen to him eventually. I get on with him, but I detest the way he treats women, all women. Dara, I'm sorry for what he's put you through over the years. Please find it in your heart to forgive him— he's a confused man, who often neglects to think of right and wrong. His 'brain' dangling between his legs makes too many of his decisions. Sometimes I find myself ashamed to call him my brother. Please rethink your actions before things get out of hand. For all our sakes, don't stoop to his level."

Felicity applauded. "Bravo. You've summed up the situation perfectly, David. It won't make the slightest difference, though, at least not in your brother's case—"

"But, Felicity," Dara interrupted, "you said—you *promised* me that you wouldn't hurt him."

Felicity cackled and smiled at her friend. "I lied."

Dara's legs gave way, and Mags and Julie rushed forward to support her.

"No! Please, I don't want any harm to come to him. I love him!"

"Don't be so pathetic, Dara. How can you love a man like that? You disappoint me. Go, get out of my sight. I can't stand the sound of your whimpering and foolish words."

"But…"

"Take her in the other room, girls. Let us get on with our work."

Mags and Julie whisked the sobbing Dara from the room. She called over her shoulder once more, "Jordan, forgive me. I had no idea this was going to happen. *No* idea."

Felicity watched the snarl on Jordan's face. "I don't believe you, Dara. Whatever these women have planned for me, it'll be nothing compared to what I'll do to you when I get my hands on you."

Disgusted by his boldness, Felicity shook her head and bent over to whisper in his ear, "If you get out of this alive!"

CHAPTER SIX

That day and the next, Lorne found herself mired in frustration. The case of the man stabbed with a high-heel was a perplexing one that offered up very little to investigate. Katy shooed Lorne out of the office early that afternoon to ensure she made it to the TV station in time for the interview.

Lorne rushed home, checked that Onyx was ready and looking her best for the camera, then ran upstairs to shower and change into a comfortable pair of trousers and a blouse. She was aiming for a smart but casual ensemble, nothing too fancy for the TV slot.

"Are you coming with me, Charlie?"

"Wow, really? Nothing like giving me a little notice, Mum? Have I got time to have a shower?"

"Sorry, I should have mentioned it sooner. Run along. I think we should take the pups, too. I think we'll gain more sympathy votes, don't you?"

Tony poured hot water into two coffee mugs. "That's a great idea. I'll stay here and keep an eye on the other dogs. I hope we don't get bombarded with phone calls tonight."

"Why? I thought that was the whole idea of the interview—that and finding Onyx's despicable owner."

"I don't mind getting calls during the day, but at night, I want some form of peace, Lorne."

She sensed Tony wasn't being completely truthful with her. She glanced at the clock on the wall—five minutes before she and Charlie would need to start loading the dogs into the car. They hardly had enough time to begin a serious chat. "Is something wrong, love?"

"Not really. I do think we need to sit down and have a chat, though. Perhaps when you get back? I know that's not fair on you. You've had a long day, and it isn't finished yet."

She closed the distance between them and stood on tiptoe to kiss him. "We'll chat later, whether I'm flaked out or not, love, if it's that important. Should I be worried? You're not going to ask for a divorce, are you?" she joked, expecting him to laugh, but he didn't. *Oh, crap!*

He passed her a mug of coffee and kissed the tip of her nose. "We'll talk later. I hope the interview goes well."

"I do love you. You know that, right? I'm sorry if I don't show it enough."

"Hey, where's that coming from? I know you love me as much as I love you. It's just…"

Charlie thundered down the stairs, putting a stop to the conversation. "Come on, Mum. We haven't got time for a cuppa."

"Hush now," Tony said. "You go and get the dogs ready and let your mum drink her coffee in peace. There's plenty of time."

"He's right. Let me drink at least half a mug, love. I'll be out in a mo."

A disgruntled Charlie marched out the back door.

Lorne looked up into her husband's eyes once again. "And we will have a long discussion later. You hear me? The last thing I want is another marriage going off the rails. I'd rather thrash things out before they go that far, hon."

"You're reading too much into a little statement. Our marriage is far from in jeopardy, Lorne. Stop worrying."

He kissed her again, then she took a few more sips of the hot liquid and walked out the back door. Stopping on the threshold, she turned to blow him a kiss and mouthed, "I love you."

He pretended to catch the kiss in his hand.

Charlie had loaded everything but the dogs into the car by the time Lorne got outside. "I'll grab Onyx if you can put the pups in the carrier. There'll be no chance of the little mites falling all over the place in the back and slipping into a crevice."

"Aww… Onyx won't like being separated from the young ones."

"She'll be fine. They'll still be together in the back."

Lorne held out a piece of chicken to the mother dog, who took it and licked her lips. Lorne stroked and made a fuss of her for a few seconds then lifted her, tugging the T-shirt into place so the dog's flaky skin was covered and not liable to rub against her own clean clothes as she carried Onyx out to the car. Onyx whimpered once she was out of range of her pups but calmed down again when Charlie arrived with the carrier and put the pups next to her in the back of the rescue centre's van.

The drive into London took longer than expected due to the rush-hour traffic, and Lorne and Charlie arrived in the TV station car park with two minutes to spare.

"Quick, or we'll miss our cue," Charlie said, being impatient as only a teenager could.

"I'm going as quickly as I can. Grab the pups. I'll bring Onyx."

"All right. I know what to do. I'm not stupid, Mum."

Lorne rolled her eyes towards the sky. *Less attitude, Charlie. More speed.*

They ran into the reception area, where a stressed-out young woman awaited their arrival.

"I'm so sorry. The traffic was really bad."

"You're here now," she replied tersely. "Come with me."

Lorne and Charlie trotted behind the woman marching down the corridor ahead of them.

"She seems pretty pissed off, Mum," Charlie said out the corner of her mouth.

"Yeah, let's make sure we don't make her mood any worse, all right?" She pleaded silently for her daughter to rein in her petulance.

"Spoilsport."

In spite of herself, Lorne chuckled. When she realised the studio was directly ahead of them, Lorne felt her nerves kick in. The interviewer introduced himself as Mike Green. He took one look at Onyx and shrank back in his chair. Lorne wondered if she'd done the right thing by bringing the poor girl.

"So, this is how things will go. I'll introduce you. Then you tell me a little about what you do, you know, your role in saving these animals. Then we'll move on to the dog. Does it have a home to go to yet?"

Lorne ground her teeth in irritation of the man's lack of compassion. "The *dog* is called Onyx. She's had a rough start in life, Mr. Green. Let's try and not hold that against her when talking about her if we can, eh? Dogs have feelings, as all animals do. They sense people's negativity towards them from the outset."

"I'm sorry. It wasn't intentional. It's just a little off-putting to see her in that state, that's all. No offence meant."

"Well, this *state,* as you call it, was caused by humans. She didn't have a lot of say in that. Maybe I should reconsider doing the interview if you can't bear the thought of being in the same room as her. You look utterly disgusted by her appearance—that is not what I expected at all when I was invited to come here."

The man's chin nearly hit the floor. He looked shocked that someone should speak to him in such a way. However, Lorne wasn't about to let someone like him look down his nose at either her or an animal she was trying her hardest to save.

"I'm sorry. It's just…"

"Two minutes to air, people." A man with headphones looped around his neck approached Green and Lorne. He bent down to stroke Onyx. "What an adorable creature. You poor baby. You're in desperate need of a good home, aren't you, sweetie? If only I wasn't out of the house all day, I'd offer to give her a happy home."

"Thank you. I appreciate your kind words. She's a very gentle soul in need of a forever home where someone could lavish her with love twenty-four-seven until she regains her trust in mankind." Lorne glanced up at Mr. Green, who appeared to be seething at the way his colleague was fussing over the stray. "Luckily, Mr. Green, there are still compassionate people left in this world. Let's hope the interview will help find Onyx a caring individual willing to look past her tortured body."

The man with the headset answered for him, "Oh, we'll certainly do our best. This sweet girl needs to be spoilt, not ill-treated the way she has been. Look at those eyes—she's too adorable for words. Do your best, Mike. Let's find this pup a good home tonight."

Seconds later, the camera rolled, and they were on air. When the red light glowed on the camera, Mike swung into action, and his behaviour towards the dog changed immediately.

"I'm here tonight with Lorne Warner, who runs a small rescue centre for abandoned dogs. Unfortunately, she's brought along a stray that has probably had the hardest life imaginable. Why don't you tell us Onyx's story, Lorne?"

"Well, she was found in Golders Park down by the boating lake, along with her four pups, which someone had tied up in a black bag."

"Oh, my goodness, how terrible." Mr. Green looked genuinely disgusted. Maybe his colleague had had a hand in changing his mind. "So, you took her in. Are you looking for a new home for Onyx?"

"Not at the moment. She has a condition called demodectic mange, and she's under the vet's care for the next month or so. Onyx needs a lot of care and regular baths right now. That wouldn't be fair to a new owner to take on that kind of responsibility. I have to say that her skin has improved over the last few days, so the signs are good that she's going to make a full recovery and be available for adoption very soon."

"Did the authorities look for the previous owner?"

"That's where the general public comes into play. If anybody recognises the dog, they can call the centre and give the owner's name in the strictest of confidence. The person probably doesn't even realise he's committed a criminal act, or maybe he does. Let's try and work together and get this person arrested on animal cruelty charges that come with either a heavy fine or a prison sentence attached. Those charges are nothing, however, compared to the pain and suffering Onyx has suffered at her owner's hands. The vet's bills alone are crippling to a small rescue centre such as ours. Therefore, I'm desperate to get the justice Onyx deserves."

"So this condition cannot just appear overnight. Is that what you're saying?"

"Oh, no. Onyx has been suffering with this condition for months. The thing that worries me is that she's obviously been with another dog for her to have had babies. The question is, does the male dog live with Onyx's previous owner, who dumped Onyx and her pups, or was he roaming the streets? Onyx was not a *lost* dog. Someone put her babies in a bag. Someone out there must know something about this. Please get in touch. I think you have the number, Mike, yes?"

"I do. We'll get that up on the screen now. I urge you nice people out there to ring this number with any information you have regarding this cute dog, Onyx. And if anyone is willing to give her and her pups a home in the future, they should also ring the same number."

"That's right." Lorne opened the carrier at her feet and took out one of the tan puppies, holding it up to the camera. "We're always on the lookout for kind people to adopt our dogs. We make every effort to ensure our dogs don't end up back on the streets. If people are okay with that, then I urge them to go ahead and dial the number. These little guys won't be ready to rehome for at least another two or three weeks, though."

"But if anyone is hoping to give another dog a new home, they should also call you. I bet there are other adorable dogs in residence with you who need homes right now."

"There are. At the moment, we have ten other dogs searching for forever homes. They come in all shapes and sizes, from Jack Russells to German shepherds and everything in between."

"Thanks for coming in today, for making us aware of this issue. I'd like to thank you personally for the great job you and your family are doing to save these animals and the work you do finding them caring homes for the rest of their lives."

Lorne smiled, amazed at the turnaround in the man's compassion. "I appreciate you allowing us to make our plea today. Thank you."

The interviewer finished up the session and went to the ad break. He shook Lorne's hand. "I'm sorry for being so abrupt with you at the beginning. Put it down to nerves. I hope you find the bastard who did this. I truly do."

"Thank you. I understand completely. I couldn't do your job as I suspect you'd have a hard time doing mine."

"Didn't someone say you're a serving officer in the Met? How do you manage both careers?"

"I am. My daughter runs the rescue centre alongside my husband. I would be lost without their help. I left the Met a few years ago and set up the business, but I got drawn back in—I missed the force too much. I didn't want to mention that on air. Was that all right?"

"Of course. Oh, well, we better get you out of here and back home. Can you manage?"

"I can. Thanks again. I'll let the station know what kind of response we get, if that's okay?"

"Brilliant, maybe we can do a follow-up interview in a few months. Maybe we could even do a regular slot for you, to help re-home your dogs. I know our sister station in America does something similar with a lot of success."

"Sounds fantastic. I'll be in touch soon."

Charlie and Lorne left the studio, each in a buoyant mood.

"That was fun, eventually. I wish we could turn everyone's attitude around like that. Let's hope some good comes from it."

"He was a bit of a pr... pratt," Charlie said, correcting the name she was going to call Mr. Green. "Do you think he was just spinning you a line about doing a regular show?"

"Only time will tell. Let's head home."

When they arrived home, Tony's expression didn't do a good job of hiding how harassed he was. Running a hand through his greying hair, he said, "The darn phone hasn't stopped ringing all night. I thought we'd get bombarded with a few calls, but this is just ridiculous."

The house phone started ringing.

"Grr… see what I mean? Well, I've had enough. You two can handle them from now on. I'm out of here." He stomped across the kitchen, swept up the car keys Lorne had just placed on the table, and walked out the back door.

Panicked about their brief conversation before she'd left for the TV station, Lorne raced after him, issuing instructions for Charlie to answer the call and then to put the answerphone on.

"Tony, please, don't go."

"Don't try and stop me. I've had enough for one day. I need to get out of here."

"I'll come with you then. We can go for a drink down the pub and have that chat?"

Tony slumped against the car door and folded his arms. "I don't mind. What about Charlie and this place?"

"She'll be fine, I've ensured everywhere is locked up, and I've told her to put the answerphone on."

"Doh! Why didn't I think of that? Okay, a drink sounds just what I need."

The five-minute journey to the pub was conducted in silence, while Lorne wondered what lay ahead of her.

Lorne chose a small intimate table in the bay window of the pub while Tony went to order their drinks at the bar. He joined her with a pint of bitter for himself and a vodka and coke for her.

"Do you want to tell me what's wrong, love? It's not like you to go off in a huff like that." She reached across the table and gathered his hand in hers.

"I just flipped."

She smirked. "I can see that. Why?"

"The simple answer is, I've had enough, Lorne."

"Of what? Us?"

His gaze connected with hers, and his eyes filled with tears. This was totally out of character for him, and the thought of him being about to tell her their marriage was over made her heart skip several beats.

Her anxiety mounted with every passing second he delayed his answer, prompting her to squeeze his hand. "Tony, be honest with me now. Cards on the table, love."

Tony untangled his hand from hers and gulped down half his pint then wiped his mouth. "We're fine. It's just me."

Lorne flinched. She'd said the very same words to her first husband when she'd finally plucked up the courage to ask for a divorce. She closed her eyes, squeezing back tears. She couldn't bear the thought of losing Tony, her soul mate. She'd spent half her life searching for him. She couldn't—and wouldn't—lose him. She opened her eyes to find him staring at her with his head tilted, looking like an inquisitive owl.

"What exactly do you mean by that, love?"

"What it says on the tin, I guess. I need more to life than this."

He wasn't making it easy for her at all. She couldn't tell if he was trying to end their marriage gently. She bit down hard on her tongue and waited for him to continue.

"You have your job, Lorne. You're fulfilled every day of the week. You're challenged day in day out when you're trying to solve your cases. What do I have?"

"Oh, love, we spoke about this before my return to the Met. We did discuss it. Didn't we?"

"Yes. I hold my hands up high. I was the one pushing you to return to the force. I admit that. I never dreamed I would feel the way I do after only a few short months."

"What are you saying? That you want me to give up my job?"

"No. Not at all. What I'm trying to say is that I need to feel the same genuine fulfilment you have at the end of the day, or week even. Do you understand that? I need to get myself a job."

"Of course I do. But what about your leg?"

"What about it? The specialist says that the prosthetic leg has finally settled down. And I concur—I no longer feel detached from my own body, if I can phrase it like that-"

Lorne winced. "I wouldn't have put it quite like that myself, but, hey, that's called making progress, isn't it? It's the work side of things hampering your fulfilment, not us?"

He took her hand in both of his and kissed the back of it. "No, it's not *us*. There is absolutely nothing wrong with us. In fact, if it's at all possible, I think I can honestly say that I love you more and more each day. Is that too cliché?"

"It might be, but I adore hearing it. Phew, what a relief. I thought our marriage was in serious trouble for a minute there. So, it's the rescue centre that's getting you down?"

"Yes, I hate to bring it up, love. However, this was all your dream."

"I know." She lowered her head in shame. "I realise it wasn't fair to burden you with my business. At the time, we both agreed it would be a good idea. Money was tight. That's why I went back to the Met and took the demotion, if you like."

He placed a finger under her chin, forcing her to look him in the eye. "I know you sacrificed a lot. You gained a lot, too, like self-esteem."

"Oh, Tony, I thought you were happy. This has all come as a shock to me. So, what's the answer? How do we get your life back on track? Close the centre down. Is that really the answer?"

"No, I'm not saying that at all. Charlie is more than capable of running that place by herself. I could still do the odd maintenance job when needed. I wouldn't run out on you totally. I was wondering—you'll probably laugh at the suggestion—if I could take over your role in the PI business."

Lorne collapsed back in her chair. "What? You'd really want to do that? What about the danger?"

His left eyebrow hitched up, à la Roger Moore. Although when he spoke again, he sounded more like Sean Connery. "You're talking to an ex-MI6 operative, young lady. Danger is, sorry *was*, my middle name."

Lorne laughed. "Another cliché?"

"Maybe a tiny one." He laughed with her. "Do you fancy something to eat?"

"Yikes, I forgot I hadn't eaten. I'll share a bowl of chips with you, unless you want something more?"

"No, I ate earlier. I'll order some chips to nibble on." He rose from the table and bent down to kiss her forehead. "Although, given the opportunity, I'd rather nibble on you." His comment earned him a swipe on the backside when he walked towards the bar.

She watched him in awe, thankful that she had avoided a devastating announcement. Thinking back over the months, if she were totally honest about things, she had seen the signs long ago, but she'd been so wrapped up in her cases that she had chosen to ignore things she should have confronted. She narrowed her eyes at him.

"What's that look for?" he asked, rejoining her.

"You think I'm stupid, don't you?"

His hand covered his chest, and he winked at her. "*Moi*, think you stupid. Never!"

"I should have realised what would happen the second you got involved in one of my bloody cases. It was that run to France that did it, wasn't it? Your help getting those ghastly men of Luigi's back, that's the real reason behind your change of heart, yes?"

"You got me. It made me feel worthwhile again, if you can understand what I'm getting at? I didn't enjoy playing my part in that case just because Luigi and Jade are family. It was to rid the streets of scum like that. I've been mulling things over ever since. You can't hold that against me."

"Sweetheart, I totally understand where you're coming from. Honest, I do. Why don't we have a sit down chat with Charlie over the weekend?"

"Sounds great."

"She's going to love running the place on her own. I know someone else who'd relish getting involved, too."

His brow furrowed. "Who?"

"Carol. I think she's doing less and less psychic work now. She's always hinting that she would love to help out now and again. This will be her chance to jump on board. We could come to some payment arrangement, I'm sure. In fact, she'll probably tell us to forget it."

"Good call. I think she'd be happy about the opportunity, too."

The barman placed a bowl of chips on the table between them.

"We'll find out what Charlie thinks about it later. I'm starving. Dig in."

Lorne sighed in relief. She much preferred Tony leaving the business to him leaving her. Her life would end if Tony ever walked out on her.

CHAPTER SEVEN

Lorne breezed into work the next day to find Katy chatting and flirting with AJ at his desk. "Morning, both of you. What a beautiful day it is today."

"Get your oats last night, Lorne?" AJ asked cheekily.

She could do very little about the colour rising in her cheeks. "No. Did you?" she retorted, surprising herself, as well as everyone else present. She chuckled, but no one else did. "Anything new regarding the Alder case?"

"Nope, except..." AJ searched a pile of papers on his desk then held up a scrap of paper. "This caught my eye when I arrived first thing." He winced at Katy. "Sorry, I forgot to mention it."

"Other things on your mind, AJ?" Lorne teased, to her own amusement again.

With a creased brow, Katy took the paper from his hand. "I'm not sure I understand what you're getting at, AJ."

"Okay, I didn't at first, either. Look at the address."

Katy passed the paper to Lorne. "Killington Industrial estate. Sorry, I'm still at a loss. What about it, AJ?"

"Thinking outside the box, I'm kind of making a loose connection to the Don Alder case. He was found about a mile away from there, wasn't he?"

"Yes, he was." Lorne's head tilted as she thought. "But then, we're talking about the London area here, AJ. Just how many crimes do you think happen in a radius of a mile or two every week?"

"I see your point, but you're totally missing something here, Lorne. Look at the other details."

"Two men reported missing, possibly *missing*." She glanced up at him, and something began to tick over in her mind. "I'm seeing a faint connection. You seriously think it's worth checking up on?"

Katy answered for him, "What other leads do we have? I can't spend another day sitting around here, twiddling my thumbs. Can you?"

Lorne shook her head, thinking she would detest another day like the previous one. "Maybe we should head out there? At least ask some questions? Who knows where it will lead? Like you say, we've got nothing better to fill our time at present."

"Okay, let's grab a quick coffee. I'll deal with any emergency post, and then we'll head out. How's that sound?" Katy levered herself off AJ's desk and crossed the room to her office.

"I'll bring the coffee in," Lorne called after her.

"Sorry, did I miss out that particular instruction?"

Lorne shook her head. "Cheeky mare. Seriously, anything you want to tell me about last night, AJ?"

From the depths of her office, Katy bellowed, "I can still hear you, and I'm not hearing any footsteps approaching the coffee machine yet."

Lorne laughed. "She can see through walls, too. We'll chat more later."

AJ motioned for her to lean in then whispered conspiratorially, "Don't bother. There's nothing to tell anyway."

She patted the back of his hand. "Sorry, hon. Maybe soon. I better get that drink into her."

Within the hour, Lorne and Katy pulled up outside the accountancy firm who had placed the call about two of their associates going missing.

The secretary greeted them with a well-practiced smile pulling at her lips. "Good morning, ladies. What can I do for you today?"

The detectives offered up their IDs. "Can we see the person in charge? It's concerning a call we received yesterday."

"Of course. Take a seat for a second if you like." The secretary swiftly disappeared through the door behind her then returned moments later with a smart-looking gentleman in his early sixties.

He introduced himself and shook hands. "Mr. Gordon. Thank you for coming out so promptly. Shall we go through to my office? Would you like a drink?"

They declined the drink and followed him through the office door.

"This is all rather perplexing, ladies. I'm not entirely sure what to think about it all."

Lorne took out her notebook and left Katy to ask the initial questions.

"What can you tell us, Mr. Gordon? Perhaps the names of the men involved?" Katy asked.

"They're brothers. Jordan and David Calleja."

"That's a strange surname. I take it they're foreign?"

"Yes, they originate from Malta, but they've been residents and working in this country for the past twenty years, I believe. So they're not part of the recent influx of immigrants."

"Are you suggesting that something has happened to them because they're foreign?" Katy asked, looking perplexed.

"No, not at all. I just presumed that would be your next question. Sorry for jumping ahead."

"No worries. Can you tell us what has raised your suspicions that something untoward has happened to the brothers?"

"Well, for a start, the brothers have always been punctual and ever present at the firm since they started here. They never ring in sick or take time off they shouldn't take."

"I see. Have you questioned the staff at all? Maybe one of the brothers said something to an associate, intimating they were about to leave the firm. Is that possible?"

The man bounced back in his high-backed executive chair. "Goodness, no. We've recently held talks about the two brothers investing in the firm. Why would they just take off and leave?"

Lorne looked up from her notes. "Maybe they thought they could do better by branching out on their own. It's not implausible, is it?"

"Actually, it is, grossly implausible. They're men of honour. If they agree with something in principle, then they usually follow through with that particular scheme. Then there's the matter of their families, of course."

"What do you mean, Mr. Gordon?" Katy asked.

"I rang them the second the men didn't show up for work yesterday. David's wife hadn't heard from him, and Jordan's, umm… girlfriend, shall we say, hadn't heard from him, either. Again, that's very unusual."

"I see. Would you be kind enough to give us the ladies' addresses? We'll call around to get a statement from both of them after we're finished here."

"I'll get my secretary to dig out the details for you."

"So neither the wife nor girlfriend has seen either man since when?"

"Two days ago."

"Okay, and when was the last time one of your colleagues saw them?"

"Approximately six p.m. the previous evening."

"That's the usual time for them to leave?"

Mr. Gordon nodded.

Katy continued, "So is it possible someone could have been waiting for them to leave?"

"In the car park? I never thought about that. But why would someone attack them?"

"That's what we intend to find out, Mr. Gordon. I don't suppose you have any CCTV footage on site, do you?"

His shoulders slumped, and he thumped his head with the heel of his hand. "Of course we do. It just never occurred to me to view the discs."

"Mind if we take a look at them now?"

"No, come this way please?"

The three of them went back through the reception area and into a tiny office at the end of the corridor. They squeezed into the room while Mr. Gordon set up the disc.

"I'll just whizz through to find the right time," he said.

At two minutes to six, one of the men walked across the car park.

"Wait, what's this?" Mr. Gordon pointed to a woman getting out of a car.

Lorne's and Katy's eyes bulged when they looked at each other.

"Female," Lorne mouthed to her partner.

Katy nodded.

CHAPTER EIGHT

The two detectives watched the footage for another couple of minutes, intrigued to see another man join the first man and woman, closely followed by a whole group of women who went on to surround the second man.

"Who is that? The two brothers?" Lorne asked.

"Yes. Although I have no idea who the women are. I've never seen them before. I could ask around the rest of the staff to see if anyone recognises them, if that would help."

"Thank you, we need to establish that at least in advance of beginning our enquiries."

Mr. Gordon disappeared, and as soon as he was out of earshot, Lorne pointed at the screen and whispered, "The men don't seem in distress or any trouble to me. What about you?"

"I was just thinking the same. It just looks as though they're involved in a friendly conversation. If the staff has no knowledge of who these women are, then I'm really not sure where we should go from here. Dare I say the brothers appear to be enthusiastic about being in the women's company? Maybe they were offered sex on a plate, and it lasted longer than expected. Like a few days longer."

"You think? Would a group of women really just turn up like that and offer sex on a plate? Not something I've heard of before."

The sound of voices approaching halted their conversation. Mr. Gordon introduced the other three members of staff and asked them if they recognised anyone on the fourteen-inch screen.

Gordon's three colleagues all shook their heads, dismayed that they couldn't help. Reluctantly, Mr. Gordon shrugged and sent them back to their offices. "I'm sorry, detectives."

"We'll make some preliminary enquiries and talk to the brothers' other halves, but observing the reaction of the men, we've come to the conclusion that they don't appear to be in any imminent danger. Therefore, I'm afraid we cannot attach any great urgency to the case. Most of our cases concern murder victims, Mr. Gordon."

"Then why are you here? I informed the police that two of my associates were missing, not murdered."

"I agree—it was our mistake. We're investigating a crime that took place in the area and might have been linked to the disappearance of your colleagues. There appears to be no such connection. I'll leave you my card. If neither of the brothers turn up within—what time limit shall we give? A week?" Katy asked.

Lorne nodded. "Sounds good to me."

"A week it is then. I'll ring you next week if you haven't contacted us before then. If the brothers should show up in the meantime, please ring me immediately."

"I will. This is all such a mystery. Tell me, detectives, do you believe in gut instinct?"

"We do. At least my colleague does." Katy threw a thumb in Lorne's direction. "Why?"

"I just know that something very wrong has occurred. Just what that is, I simply can't begin to tell you. However, I know neither of the Calleja brothers would lose contact with their families *and* the firm. Their diaries are full, important meetings scheduled for the rest of the week. I can't emphasise that enough. I'm asking you to take their disappearance very seriously."

"You have my assurance that will be the case once the men have been missing a reasonable length of time." Katy walked towards the door.

"Here's my card. You hold up your end of the bargain, and I'll hold up mine, okay?" Mr. Gordon said.

"Thank you. Let's hope the men show up soon. In the meantime, can you give us their home addresses? We'll make tentative enquiries to begin with. Hopefully, something will come from them. Thanks for contacting us. We'll be in touch either way, soon. Goodbye, Mr. Gordon."

Katy and Lorne shook hands with the man and left. After taking a quick scout around the car park to look for clues, they drove to the first address.

A woman in her mid-to-late thirties opened the door, her eyes bloodshot and red-rimmed.

"Mrs. Calleja? I'm DI Katy Foster, and this is my partner, DS Lorne Warner. We've been asked to look into your husband's disappearance. Mind if we come in?"

"Of course." She led them through to a lounge filled with antique wood furniture and invited them to sit on the sofa.

Again, Katy asked the questions while Lorne took down the woman's answers. "First of all, I have to ask if you and your husband were having any difficulties in your marriage?"

Her hand flew up to her chest. "No. Never. David and I live a wonderful life, never a cross word between us. We love each other, have done since our teens."

"I see." Katy paused.

Lorne could tell Katy was struggling with how to word her next question, so she jumped in. "Does your husband have any other female members of the family living close by, perhaps?"

"No. they all live in Malta. They visit often, but no one has come over to see us for at least six months. Why do you ask?"

Lorne and Katy glanced at each other, both aware of how the woman was likely to react to the news.

Katy found her voice again. "It's just that we've viewed the footage from the CCTV discs at your husband's firm, and it would appear that he drove off with a woman he met in the car park."

Mrs. Calleja jumped out of her seat as if someone had set it ablaze. She paced the floor in front of them for a few seconds then crossed the room and picked up the gold-plated framed photo of herself with her husband. She ran a finger down his face. "Not David. He wouldn't do that to me. He loves me."

"Both my partner and I witnessed the proof, not twenty minutes ago, Mrs. Calleja."

"Maria. Please call me Maria." She returned the photo to the sideboard, but instead of standing it upright, she placed the picture facedown on the wood then took up pacing once more.

"Maria, please don't get yourself worked up about this. From what we could see, the interaction between the woman and your husband seemed quite amicable."

Oops, wrong choice of words there, Katy! "What my partner is trying to do is reassure you in saying we don't believe that your husband is in danger at all."

"Oh, I see. Well, that hasn't really put my mind at rest. What about Jordan? He's missing, too. Do you know if that happened at the same time?"

Katy nodded. "It would appear so, yes." She inhaled a large breath and added, "Actually, this is not going to sound too good to your ears, apparently your husband and his brother left the area with a group of women."

"What? Is this some kind of joke?" she asked, her voice thickening with a strong Mediterranean accent.

"No, I'm afraid it's the truth. Which is why I asked if you had any female relatives living in the proximity. Any idea who these women could be? We witnessed no animosity between them. Everything seemed all very friendly, leading us to come to the conclusion that they were acquainted with them."

"But David doesn't know any women in the area. Of course." She snorted and held out her arms to the side, releasing them so they slapped her thighs. "If you're referring to Jordan, well, that would be a different ball game entirely. He has an atrocious reputation with women. His girlfriend won't be able to back me up on that point because she's only just started seeing him."

"How long?"

"In the last three to four months. Yes, they've moved in together, but David and I know that won't last. Jordan's relationships never do. His relationship with Dara is the longest he's ever stayed with a woman, because she let him get away with things. He cheated regularly behind her back. She was just too dumb to realise it. Foolish woman."

"As a matter of interest, do you have this Dara's contact details? Can you describe her for us?"

Maria marched over to the bureau and opened it. She flipped open an address book, wrote an address and phone number down, then gave it to Lorne.

"Thank you. That's a big help. And her description?"

Maria sat in the chesterfield easy chair and thought. "It's been a while since I saw her, maybe a year or two, so she might have changed. Of course, her height wouldn't change. She was around five foot three, slim build, with short-cropped hair. She wore those huge glasses that woman on Coronation Street wears—what's her name?"

Lorne remembered seeing the soap once or twice and knew one of the characters was famous for the glasses she wore. "Deirdre?" she offered hopefully.

"Yes, that's the one," Maria agreed.

"Can you tell us why they broke up? Who ended the relationship, him or her?"

"Jordan ended it. Dara came home from work early one day and found him in bed with a teenage girl."

"Ouch, that must have hurt. Is she the vindictive type? I mean, would she set out to get revenge? It's not unheard of today for many women to take that route."

Maria's mouth pulled down at the sides. "Not Dara. She's the meek and mild type. I was surprised that she didn't try to end her life after their marriage disintegrated. She always seemed the needy type to me."

Lorne knew the type only too well: the total opposite to her, the type who would generally end up surrounding themselves with animals rather than get involved with another member of the opposite sex for fear of another man breaking her heart.

"I think we can rule out her involvement then. Is there anything you can tell us about your husband's business?"

Maria raised an inquisitive eyebrow. "In what way? He's an accountant. What is there to tell?"

"Could he possibly have some dodgy clients who did business with him here after work rather than go through legitimate means via the firm? That's not unheard of."

"David would never do anything underhanded like that, either in his own country or in England. The risk of him being expelled would be enough for him to refuse such a suggestion."

Katy thought over Maria's response then quickly asked, "What about Jordan? He sounds an unsavoury character. Could he be involved in something illegal or have pulled David into an unscrupulous deal, perhaps? I'm clutching at anything and everything here. You understand, don't you?"

"I understand. Jordan has his faults, but I think his business acumen could never be questioned. Where will you start your investigation now? How long before we hear some news?"

"As we've just informed your husband's colleagues, this case won't be regarded as a priority just yet. If, however, the women had attacked the men in the car park, well, that would have been a different story entirely. It's puzzling that everything seemed amicable between the men and women, and yet, the men haven't been heard from or seen since that day."

"Please, please, you must look for my husband. He's a gentle man. He'd never hurt anyone either on purpose or by mistake. I want him back. I'm lost without him. I don't work. Without his money to pay the bills, I will have to return to Malta shortly. We have no savings I can use to live on. It's expensive to live in London, no?"

"I think we can all agree on that one," Lorne mumbled.

Katy stood up to leave, and Lorne followed her to the front door. Turning to face the distraught woman, Katy said, "We'll be in touch soon, I hope. If David shows up, please contact me on this number as soon as possible." Katy shook the woman's hand and gave her a business card.

"Well, I can see us getting nowhere fast here," Lorne said once they were back in the car.

"Makes a change, doesn't it?"

Lorne scratched her head and tried to think of suggestions, but fell flat. "The only thing we have is the cars. I know how much we're reliant on CCTV footage nowadays, but what else have we got? I'd ring the station, get AJ searching the CCTV footage at both scenes."

Katy shook her head. "On this case, I think we'll be wasting our time. For a start, we have no indication how Alder's body got to the hospital. Was it by car? Or was he attacked as he walked the street?"

Lorne stared ahead of her. "Unless we know that, we've got nothing else to go on except we think the perpetrator is a female. That's another avenue we need to start taking seriously, agreed? Is it a coincidence that the Calleja brothers were seen leaving their firm with a group of women and that Alder was suspected of being killed by a woman? Maybe we should start digging through old cases, see if anything shows up? What if we have a case of abduction going on here? Is it conceivable that Alder's abduction went horribly wrong because of the heart attack? That's my line of thinking anyway."

"Maybe you have a point. Let's visit Jordan Calleja's other half and then make our way back to the station to start delving."

"Okay. Would you like me to ring AJ, get him on the CCTV discs while you drive?" Lorne asked, removing her mobile from her jacket pocket.

"Good idea."

Lorne made the call and spent the rest of the journey searching for other angles they could try. In the end, the trip to see Jordan's partner turned out to be wasted time. The house was empty, and enquiring with the neighbours proved fruitless. No one had seen the woman since the night before.

* * *

The restless women started to bicker amongst themselves. Felicity clearly hadn't thought this side of things through well enough. She was on the verge of pulling her hair out. *What is wrong with these women? Have they had all their decision-making skills knocked out of them by the male gender?*

What should have been simple decisions took hours of debate—hours and hours. And still no conclusion. When the mission had commenced, Felicity hadn't intended on losing her self-control. However, the women's constant mithering was doing her head in. Unlike the others, who had taken the opportunity to catnap when the men had finally calmed down and shut up, Felicity hadn't slept a wink the previous night—she couldn't. Her mind was more active than a million worker bees collecting nectar from a thousand flowering shrubs.

Because of the women's arguing, Felicity had decided she was in the mood to dish out some punishment, and as they had two men wearing fetching ironmongery, they were a good place to start. The morning had started out well—not for the men but for her. Jordan had refused to eat the cereal she'd offered. So Felicity had forced it down his neck, bending his head back and covering him with the breakfast when he clamped his mouth shut. Dara had pleaded and pulled at her arms to stop her, but Felicity had shrugged off the pathetic woman. Things had progressed and had gone too far for any misgivings or changing of minds to take place. If Felicity had her way, she would kill the two men and move on to the next man on their list.

Dara and a couple of the other women had taken her aside and beseeched her to return the men to their loved ones. Felicity was certain if they let the men go, then the police would be at the cottage before anyone could wave a magic wand and cast a spell over the men. Around three a.m., she had watched the smug-looking Jordan goading her, blowing kisses in her direction. His attitude made her seek out further torture techniques to try out on him. She aimed to see the man squirm and to suffer unimaginably sadistic things, but there was little chance of that occurring if the group's behaviour was anything to go by. She would have to put her foot down and show them who was the boss. Though her role was clear, a timely reminder wouldn't do any harm.

She clapped her hands, interrupting the chatter, and called everyone to gather around. Out of the corner of her eye, she caught the stupefied expression rebounding between the two brothers. David shook in the confines of his shackles.

"Ladies, I've decided to have a little fun with our guests. Who's with me on that?"

Not a peep came from the women, although she did hear a few audible gasps from Dara.

"Dara, you're the nearest to the kitchen. Can you bring me a small sharp knife and the large carving knife please?"

The woman remained rooted to the spot. Even Julie giving her a friendly nudge with her elbow didn't shift her.

"Dara? Did you hear me?" Felicity's voice dropped into a gruff tone, clearly insinuating that she was not pleased with the woman's defiance. She scowled at the woman, and the crowd parted so that the quivering wench no longer had a hiding place.

Avoiding eye contact, Dara looked off to the left. "I can't. I won't do it. You'll have to ask someone else."

"Are you defying my orders?" Felicity boomed, loudly enough to split the stone walls of the cellar with the vibrations.

"Yes, I'm sorry. I've had enough. We've been talking, and a few of us want to set the men free. We think it has all got out of hand. Don't we, girls?"

As Felicity expected, the rest of the women remained tight-lipped. "Well? Speak up. Do we need to hold a vote?"

A few of them shook their heads whilst the others avoided eye contact with Felicity. She huffed and puffed inside, but on the surface, she continued to stay calm, allowing only her unrelenting annoyance at Dara to show. From the research she'd carried out before setting up the group, the odd person speaking out in defiance of the leader went with the territory. "Mags, how about you? Are you in or out of this next stage?"

"In, for sure." The woman had hesitated for only a split second. This pleased Felicity, especially after Dara's betrayal.

"Good. Julie? What about you?"

"I'm in," Julie replied, her mouth stretching into a somewhat grudging smile.

After that, Felicity directed one question to the rest of the women—one simple question: "In or out?"

One by one, each woman agreed.

Felicity's gaze dropped to Dara again. "You were saying? I have an awful lot of aye votes there. I didn't hear any nays. Did you, Dara?"

Dara looked crestfallen. Tears sprung to her eyes, and her head dropped. She turned on her heel, went into the kitchen, and returned with the two items Felicity had requested five minutes earlier. She walked through the crowd and placed them into Felicity's open palm.

"Thank you. Now that wasn't too difficult, was it? This might be, though. You have my permission to leave the room if you don't want to see Jordan hurt."

"Stay, Dara. Please stay," Jordan urged, out of view behind the crowd.

"He's only pleading with you for selfish reasons. He thinks I'll go easier on him if you're in the room, but I won't. I've thought long and hard about this situation. Remember why we agreed to go down this route, girls? To get revenge for the way these SOBs have treated us over the years. God made us equals in life, and equality means being treated fairly by both men and women, correct?" Felicity didn't wait for the response she knew would come. Instead, she pushed Dara aside and came face to face with David.

"No, please. I haven't done anything wrong. Spare me."

"Shut the fuck up, bro. If I get it, then so do you," Jordan vehemently told his pleading sibling.

Felicity turned to face Dara. Jabbing Jordan's temple, she asked, "Is that how he used to speak to you? In that tone? With that scowl carved into his face? Well? Is it?"

Dara gave an ashamed nod.

Felicity cupped her hand to her ear. "I can't hear you."

"Yes. Every day until he got his own way," Dara finally conceded under her leader's persistence.

"Oh, did he now? And what were the consequences if you said no?"

"It only happened the once. He beat me over the head with a broom." Dara's voice trailed off; she realised she'd just assigned her former husband's torture schedule.

"I see. Is that right, Jordan? Did you like to beat Dara?"

"Like she said, it was only the once." His brow furrowed when she clicked her fingers.

As if by magic, Julie appeared beside Felicity, holding a broom. Felicity took the wooden implement, and without even considering the consequences, she smashed the handle over his skull twice in quick succession.

The man whimpered as a lump rapidly grew through the bald patch on the top of his head. "Don't do it again. I'm begging you to have mercy on me. I apologised to Dara when I treated her so badly all those years ago. I swear I never did anything like that again."

Felicity spun around to face Dara again. "Did he?"

"No… but he did…"

"Yes, what did he do? Let me hear about all the deplorable things this man put you through. We all want to hear it. Don't we, girls?" Felicity scanned the room until everyone agreed with her.

"Thinking about it, there was one other time he really hurt me…"

"Go on, we're all listening, Dara," Felicity insisted.

"It was during sex one day. He thought it would be fun to see what it would be like to insert the end of the broom in my…"

Felicity gaped at the woman, who had buried her head in her hands. "He didn't?" She turned back to glare at the man.

Jordan appeared to be equally shocked by his former wife's confession.

Felicity suspected he knew exactly what Dara was talking about. "Did you? Did you do such a despicable thing as that, Jordan?"

"I can't remember."

"Bullshit. I can see it written on your face. Okay, I'll save that one up here." Felicity pointed to her head. "I have enough torture techniques of my own I want to try out before I get revenge for Dara on that score. Julie, are you noting this down?"

"I am. In capital letters, emphasising the severity of his crime," Julie responded, a mixture of amusement and disgust in her voice.

"Please. Dara told me she forgave me years ago for that error of judgement. All young couples experiment during sex, don't they?"

Felicity raised an eyebrow. "Only ones with warped minds like yours." She picked up the large carving knife and inched nearer to him. She tickled the soles of his feet with the cold blade. Jordan tried to pull his foot away, but the shackles around his ankles held his foot firmly in place. Felicity twisted the blade so that the edge made contact between his toes, then she pushed the point into his middle toe and dragged the blade down the length of his foot, ignoring the pitiful scream coming from his big mouth.

A thud behind her made her halt the torture. A few of the women rushed to the aid of Dara, who was lying prostrate on the stone floor. "Get her some water. Wake her up. I want her to see what I have in store for this one. I'm doing this for her benefit, after all."

Julie, a former nurse, shoved a nearby box under Dara's legs and tapped her cheeks lightly. "Wake up, hon."

"What? What went on... oh!"

"Remembered now, have we, sweetheart? *You* might have passed out, but Jordan sure didn't. Shall we try and address that?"

"No please! Look, I have money. I've been stashing it aw..." He closed his eyes, condemning his foolish loose tongue.

"Go on, don't stop there. Maybe I can take a stab at finishing that sentence for you? Let me wrack my brain and see what I can come up with. Ah yes, I've been stashing it away for years. How did I do, Jordan? By the pained expression on your face, I'd say I was spot on." Felicity's glance darted from Dara to her ex.

The woman looked on the verge of needing hospital treatment. Her cheeks had lost all colour, and her eyes were again moist with tears.

"He's not going to admit to it, Dara. I know I hit the nail on the head, though. Are you aware that he hid money from you? My guess is it's a substantial amount, too."

"No, I wasn't aware." She held out her arms for Kaz and Mags to help her to her feet. She walked over to Jordan, picked up the broom lying on the floor, and battered him over the head with it. He cried pitifully, like a child wanting his mum to come along and make everything perfect again.

There are two hopes of that happening—Bob Hope and no fucking hope.

"You disgust me. I lived hand to mouth for years with you pleading poverty at every opportunity. So, where is it? Tell me where the money is stored, and I'll plead your case with our leader to go easy on you."

"Your leader? What kind of set-up is this?"

"Don't change the subject." Dara poked his cheek.

He winced. "Don't hit me there. You know that tooth has been bad for years."

Proud of Dara for no longer taking shit from her ex, Felicity grinned, pleased another torture technique had revealed itself. She went to the pantry into the kitchen, and took out a set of her father's pliers.

"Kaz, Lenora, hold his arms. Mags, you hold his head still. Dara, do you want to do this?"

The woman's bravado faltered.

"Dara, stay strong. You can do it. Just think of the money."

That was the nudge Dara needed. She snatched the pliers from Felicity's outstretched hand and moved menacingly towards her ex. Felicity ran around the other side and rammed the end of the broom in Jordan's mouth, much to his amazement.

"Nnnnoooo!" the word came out muffled and indecipherable; it didn't take Einstein to know what the man had meant. The nearer Dara got to his open mouth, the harder it was to keep him still.

A chant broke out amongst the other women. "Do it. He deserves it. Do it. He deserves it!"

A devilish glint sparkled in Dara's eye as she lowered her head over his mouth to locate the troublesome tooth. "Well, after I've finished with you, dearest Jordan, you'll never have to visit the dentist again, except to obtain dentures maybe."

Felicity closed her eyes and stifled the laugh that caught in her throat. Lenora rushed forward to help Dara with the extraction. The crowd was silent as Dara pulled Jordan's teeth from his head and deposited them into a metal dog bowl. His cries no longer mattered. Even David's pleas for help went unnoticed.

Whether out of fear for himself or for his brother, David looked petrified and on the threshold of crapping himself. Good job he was naked. Scream after scream filled the room then faded into oblivion. Felicity took a moment to admire Jordan's resilience. He hadn't passed out during what must have been unbearable pain. *Everyone knows there's nothing worse than toothache. Still, he won't have to suffer any more after Dara has extracted his rotten teeth. I wonder what she'll move on to next, if I let her. I don't want her being greedy, spoiling all my fun!*

They would all need a rest after this exertion. David's punishment could wait until another day. The mental castigation he'd suffered would be enough to keep him in line for a few days yet. Finally, as the last tooth hit the bowl, Jordan succumbed and passed out, flopping forward and allowing the blood filling his mouth to run down and stain his legs.

Felicity chuckled. "He's going to think we've got rid of something else when he wakes up to the amount of blood in that area now."

Dara's lip curled up. "Give me time. I never thought I would ever enjoy myself inflicting pain on another human being."

"Now, don't you start feeling bad. Just think of all the times he's mistreated you over the years. Don't worry, we'll get the whereabouts of that money before…"

"Before what, Felicity?"

"We're finished with him."

Dara laughed. "Or finish him off completely. I could, you know."

"Hey, no one could ever doubt you after that performance, dear lady."

The group erupted into laughter then, and Felicity glanced sideways at David's reaction. He was quivering harder than a petrified jellyfish. *Bless him. We'll have our fun with you, buddy. Mark my words.*

She clicked her fingers to gain everyone's attention. "Our plan just grew, ladies. You've seen the fun Dara had tonight seeking her revenge. Now it's your turn. Tomorrow, I'm going to hire a minivan, and we're going to round all the men up—let me rephrase that. We're going to round up all our ex-significant others and bring them back here. How about it?"

CHAPTER NINE

Once Lorne arrived home from work that evening, she and Tony sat down at the kitchen table after dinner and sifted through the calls they'd received since the TV interview had aired. There were over forty of them. Interestingly, a couple of the callers had given the same name for Onyx's owner.

"What are the odds on that? Two different callers pointed the finger at this Gary Metcalfe. That can't be a coincidence, can it?" Lorne asked. She looked towards the back door as it inched open. "Come in."

"Hello, you two, not interrupting anything, am I?" Their psychic friend, Carol Lord, entered the room and closed the door behind her.

"Hi, Carol. Not at all. What brings you out here at this time of day? Have you eaten?"

"Don't fuss now. Yes, I've eaten. Well, I wanted to come and see if I could lend a hand. I have a feeling you could do with some extra help right now. Not sure in what respect, though."

"You're not wrong there. Did you see me on TV?" Lorne got up to turn on the kettle.

"I did. That poor pup—she looked absolutely petrified. Any news from the appeal?"

"Yes and no. We're going through what information came in now. How are things with you, Carol? Are you busy?"

Carol's eyes narrowed. "Why don't you just come out and ask me, Lorne?"

Lorne sniggered and poured boiling water into the mugs. "You're living up to your name of being one of the best psychics in the area, Carol."

"Come on, out with it. *Then* I'll tell you why I've come over here."

"That sounds ominous. You first." Lorne placed the three mugs on the table.

"No way. You first. The answer will be yes anyway. I just want to hear you ask me."

"You mean grovel," Tony corrected her then gave a laugh that earned him a dig in the ribs from Lorne.

"How much are you aware of?" Lorne asked, calling her friend's bluff.

"That Tony isn't satisfied about spending time around here rather than chasing criminals. Am I right?"

Tony eyed Lorne then winked at Carol. "Correct, Carol. So…"

The psychic held up her hand to stop him. "So, let me guess, you'd like me to help out around here. All right, I buckled under the strain, Lorne. I should have waited for you to ask, but I'm just too excited not to jump right in with both feet. I'd love to help out more. Plus, I believe Charlie and I would make a great team."

"*Seriously*? You really wouldn't mind? We couldn't afford to pay much to begin with, although you have my assurance that we won't see you go short, either. With both Tony and I working full time away from here, in the future, I'm sure that situation will be rectified soon enough if you bear with us a short time."

"Nonsense. Take your time. For now, I'll be more than willing to do it for free. You know how much I adore working and playing with dogs."

Lorne laughed. "I'll remind you about that at the end of the first week. I hear Charlie can be a harsh task master where cleaning out the kennels are concerned. Isn't that right, Tony?"

"Yeah, very harsh. Not that I want to put you off or anything." He grinned broadly.

"Well, I'm willing to give it a try if you'll have me."

Lorne went over to hug her friend. "You, dear lady, are what is commonly known as an angel in disguise."

"I know. You might want to take a seat again, love."

Lorne fell back into her chair with a heavy thud. "Okay, reveal all. What have you seen?"

"There's trouble brewing, dear. I can't quite tell you what just yet, but I fear it is connected to the case you're dealing with. Leave me a while to sort it out, and I'll tell you the news as I receive it. Now, what's all this paperwork about? The TV interview?"

"Yes. We've had about forty calls. The object of the interview was to try and find the person who dumped poor Onyx and to possibly find new homes for her and the pups."

"And? No, wait—let *me* tell you." Carol closed her eyes and rocked back and forth as she tuned into the information being fed to her by her spirit guides. Opening her eyes, she pointed at a piece of paper in front of Lorne. "There, that's her owner, vile man. There's something not quite right about him. The spirits are telling me you need to handle him with caution."

"Well, that matches what we thought. Two people contacted us and gave the same name. We were just debating that when you arrived. So, you're saying it would be a good idea to go and see him mob-handed?"

"You know I can't be more specific than that, dear. Just be aware that he's a sandwich short of a picnic and approach with care. As to a suitable home for Onyx, look no further." She pointed at her chest. "I'll have the cutie. You know she'd be well cared for and want for nothing. She could even come to work with me once I start my new job. I hear my new bosses are very understanding in that respect."

They all laughed. Lorne hugged Carol again. "You're wonderful, Carol. I'd be super happy for Onyx to have you as her new mummy. Let's keep her here for a little while, at least until her course of treatment has finished, and then you can take her home with you. How's that?"

"That's brilliant. I can help Charlie care for her here daily. That way, she'll get used to me quicker than if I dropped by and picked her up like a stranger. I know she has trust issues, and after having a telling vision about her previous owner, I can see why she finds it hard to trust humans. I hope you finally catch up with the bastard and string him up for the dreadful things he's done to that dog. I fear you're going to have a job on your hands tracking him down, though."

"Thanks for the warning. I'll get onto the RSPCA tomorrow to see if they can give me any past details on him. Maybe he's had prior warnings issued. You never know. Wait a minute—when you arrived, you mentioned you had news about the case I'm involved in. Were you talking about Onyx's case?"

Carol frowned. "No. The case you're dealing with regarding some missing men. Clues are a little light for both of us at present, I'm guessing. My spirit guides keep flinging things at me which I just wanted to pass on to you."

"Such as?" Lorne asked.

"This is going to sound totally out there, and I'm really not sure what it has to do with anything in today's world, but you need to be aware of what they're telling me. They keep showing me a huge hill—more like a mountain, I suppose—and the name Pendle or Pemble. The name's not coming across very clearly."

Lorne shrugged. "In this area? Huge mountains or hills? I suppose there would be similar kinds of landscapes right out in the countryside, but to be honest, we're looking at crimes within the London area, all within a five-mile radius of each other. That just seems bizarre to me and completely irrelevant."

"I'm just passing on the message, as usual. I'll ask you to go back to past experience, Lorne, and please just bear the information in mind when delving into the case. All right?"

"Anything else you can tell us, Carol?"

She closed her eyes again and rocked. "Only that I'm picking up some kind of cave with stone walls and shackles. That could be anything, though, couldn't it?"

"Hardly anything! Are there any caves in the area? Do you know, Tony?" Lorne glanced at her husband, who appeared to be equally perplexed.

"Along the coast, possibly. Not in the location you're looking into, love."

"See? This is what I'm up against on this one. The only piece of concrete evidence we have is that one man was attacked with a woman's stiletto heel, and the two men who have been reported as missing left their place of work willingly with a group of women."

"Can you identify the women?" Carol asked.

"They're a little too far away from the camera to make a positive ID. We couldn't quite make out the number plates of the vehicles, either."

"That's a shame. I think that will be your main clue in breaking the case."

"I'm intending to chase that up tomorrow. AJ was going to sort that side of things out for us while Katy and I were on the road today. We need to follow these two cars on the CCTV footage. It's all we have."

"For now." Carol noted cryptically.

"Are you hinting you've seen more surrounding this case?"

"Yes, I've seen more. It's all rather confusing at present. If I let you have everything at once, it could lead you down the wrong routes and delay any arrests you want to make. Just be satisfied with what I've given you so far, and we'll go from there, okay?"

"It's going to have to be okay, if you're eager to sit on the other clues," Lorne bit back harshly. "I'm sorry. That came out the wrong way. I'm just frustrated up to here right now." She held her hand flat two inches above her head.

"I understand. Bear with me. As soon as things become clearer, I'll be sure to let you know. Use the clues I have given you wisely, and they'll guide you in the end, providing you don't turn your back on them. Oh, and by the way, Tony, when you resurrect the old PI business, your help will prove to be invaluable in cracking this case."

Lorne and Tony turned to each other and shook their heads.

"Really? That's good to know we'll be working together in the near future," Tony replied, giving Lorne's hand a quick squeeze.

"We need to make a few calls before you start touting the business around. It's in my name, don't forget. I'll get it transferred. That should be easy enough to do." She raised her mug, and the three of them clicked the pottery together over the middle of the table. "To us, all of us. What an incredible team."

CHAPTER TEN

First thing at work the following morning, Lorne rang the RSPCA to make the enquiries about Gary Metcalfe, the man who she assumed to be Onyx's owner. She was disappointed that they had nothing on record for either the man or the dog, but the worker assured her that someone would be willing to look into the case. Then she asked AJ if the footage had shown up anything while they were out the previous day.

"Not so far. I followed the two cars through the town and out into the countryside. That's where it ends. Unfortunately, no CCTV cameras exist past the outskirts of the town."

Katy walked into the incident room. "Morning, folks. Any news?"

"Morning. Not really. I'd like a private chat if that's okay." Lorne smiled wearily.

"Of course, come on through. I'll grab a coffee on the way. Had the night from hell last night, regarding my folks." Katy bought them each a coffee, then they entered her office. She shut the door behind Lorne and motioned for her to take a seat opposite her own chair. "What's up?"

"I had a visit from Carol last night. That can wait, though. What's wrong with your parents? Anything I can do to help?"

"Nope, same old, same old. 'When are we going to see you?' and all that crap. You know how demanding this job is, Lorne. Why can't I make them understand how draining it is being a DI? Even at home, I'm still on the job." She prodded the side of her head. "This doesn't switch off, ever. If I'm not thinking over possible leads to a case, I'm mulling over what paperwork to finish up first when I return the next day. I haven't slept a full eight hours in months now. Between you and me, I'm exhausted, mentally and physically. How did you ever cope? You had Charlie to bring up on top of all the other shit thrown at you."

"That's just it—I didn't. Tom looked after Charlie while I was at work. Many a time, I used to say to Dad, 'There's got to be more to life than this.' The trouble is, I loved my job. Dedication drove me on, just like it will you, hon. Stick with it. Don't let your parents' moaning grind you down and force you to do something foolish that you'll regret later. I see so many comparisons in us, Katy. Don't for goodness' sake jack the job in to please others. The decision, if that's what is running through your mind, has to come from here, too." Lorne held her hand over her heart. "Look inside. You're not going to appreciate what I'm about to say next, but I'm going to say it all the same: you need support. Not around here. I mean at home, preferably from a partner who understands the type of stress you have to deal with on a daily basis."

Katy groaned. "How did I know this conversation would come back to me and AJ?"

"Because it makes sense. He adores you. Listen to your heart, Katy, and everything else will slot naturally into place. I've told you what the solution is—get AJ shifted off the team, and then you two can start a relationship, not that you haven't already." She grinned at the shocked look on her partner's face. "Deny it all you like. I know the signs of when two people are in love and made for each other."

"You're incorrigible, Lorne Warner."

"I know. That's why you love me. AJ would be a loss to the department—there's no denying that—but he can be replaced. I think he should be in line for a promotion anyway. He's got it in him to go far in the force, just like you have. All right, you've had a helping hand from your daddy but…"

"You cheeky mare! Is that really what you think? You believe all the gossip that I've had tied around my neck from day one?"

"No, I *do not*. Don't tell me you've lost your sense of humour now, too?"

"Nope. Let me think on this for a while. And yes, AJ and I have been seeing each other. And yes, I think it could be getting serious between us. Take that victorious look off your face, woman."

Lorne punched the air and shot out of the chair to hug her friend. "I'm so pleased for you." She pretended to zip her lips together. "My lips are sealed on the subject. Are you going to look into working apart?"

"Yes, we've discussed it. He's a tremendous support to me. A real gem."

"All that, and he's loaded, too. What more could a girl want?" She smirked as Katy shook her head.

"Money doesn't matter to me, Lorne. It never has done. Anyway, his father has always told AJ to pay his own way. I doubt he'll get any inheritance or other funds coming his way until his old man passes away. Yikes, that sounded awful. You know what I'm getting at, right?"

"Yeah, I understand. He has to be admired. It must have been excruciatingly hard for him over the years. I wish you guys the best of luck. If ever two people were meant to be together, it's you two."

"Right, thanks." Katy's cheeks coloured up.

"Anyway, back to business. Carol Lord paid me a visit last night. She's had several visions and wasn't sure what to make of them. She believes they're firmly connected with the case we're working on."

"Well?"

"She picked up some kind of cave or a stone-walled place, the name Pendle or Pemble, and some form of mountain or very large hill."

"Something sounds familiar with Pendle. Maybe run a search on Google for that in a sec. Is that it?"

"And shackles. Yes, that's it. Mind you, while she was there, she also told us who Onyx's owner was, too. I've followed up that lead with the RSPCA. One of their inspectors is dropping around to see him today."

"That's excellent news. Let's hope they throw the book at him. I'm not sure what to make of the clues pertaining to this case, though, Lorne. They seem a little far-fetched, don't you think?"

"Initially, that's what I thought. However, if you add what Carol said to the few clues we've stumbled across already, things do seem to go hand in hand. Shackles, women abducting the men—could these women be holding the men in some sort of cave or cellar even?"

"It's not unfeasible. For what purpose?" Katy asked.

"I don't know. *Fifty Shades of Grey* type of thing, S&M, bondage. Who knows? I'm just throwing it out there."

"Hmm... you could be right. Similar cases in this vein have come to the fore since that book hit the charts. Why don't you go check the Internet while I sort through this lot?" She picked up her large mound of post and threw it back on the desk.

After leaving Katy's office, Lorne booted up one of the computers and sat down with her coffee at the desk. Nothing of any significance showed up for Pemble, so she typed in Pendle—and *bam*! For a few seconds, her eyes were glued to the screen. She scrambled out of her chair and barged into Katy's office. "Witches!"

"What about them?" Katy asked, tilting her head.

"Pendle Hill is renowned for witches and witchcraft."

Katy bounced back in her chair. "I told you I recognised the name from somewhere. It's in Lancashire, my neck of the woods. But that's miles away. How could it be connected with a case in London?"

"You know how Carol's visions work. They come in dribs and drabs most of the time. My thinking is that maybe we're working on a witchcraft case." Lorne raked her fingertips through her hair. "God, in this day and age, is that even conceivable?"

"Are you kidding me? I would have thought that to be an unnecessary question, Lorne. *Anything and everything* can be considered conceivable nowadays. Christ, where do we start on a case like that? These women are sure to have covered their tracks well, aren't they?"

"Why don't we call the team together and bounce some ideas around?"

"Good idea. I should be free in about half an hour. Will you arrange the meeting and delve into things relating to witchcraft in the London area in the meantime? A search might throw something up. You never know."

Lorne left the office, still feeling a little shell-shocked. "Hey, guys, I've stumbled across something that is going to blow this case wide open—witches."

Mouths open, the other four members of the team turned their attention to Lorne.

Shaking his head, AJ asked, "Did I hear correct? Witches? As in dressed in black capes and pointed hats variety?"

"I'm not sure I'd go that far, AJ, but yes, that type of thing. DI Foster wants to call a meeting to discuss the findings in thirty minutes or so. Get your thinking caps on, folks."

The group's excited murmurings followed Lorne back to her desk, where she punched *London* and *witches* into Google.

She located a recent case in 2010 of a fifteen-year-old boy who had been murdered by a family member because the family thought the child was possessed by the devil. The poor boy had arrived from France to stay with relatives. One day, he wet his pants, and the man he believed to be his uncle violently tortured him until he finally broke down and admitted he was a witch in the hope that the abuse would end. The boy was placed in freezing bathwater on Christmas Day and drowned. She wiped away the tears filling her eyes. *How could anyone abuse a child like that and accuse them of being a witch? What did that say about the minds of the adults?*

This particular case related to a family from the Congo, where such beliefs were rife and punishable without question. The pathologist's report read like a gruesome scene from a horror novel. The boy had over one hundred wounds—deep cuts to his neck, head and face—and he was missing several teeth. The heart-breaking tale turned her stomach.

Katy joined the group, and Lorne stood in front of the noticeboard with the latest crime noted on it. She added the word *witchcraft*.

"Have you managed to find out any relevance to it in the area?" Katy asked.

Lorne spoke as she jotted down possible links to the case. "I found a terrible story which happened back in 2010. A fifteen-year-old boy was violently abused and later killed for being a suspected witch, all because he wet his pants."

"How terrible. Don't tell me—this family don't originate from the UK."

"Nope, the Congo. I'm always concerned when people come to this country and bring their beliefs with them. So many of their beliefs are difficult for me to relate to, and it makes my job preventing things like that harder." Lorne shuddered. "I dread to think how many of these crimes are disguised in some way by the perpetrators. I bet London, and the rest of the UK for that matter, has witchdoctors and the likes in several communities. Oh, don't get me started… back to what we do know. Like I said, I don't think the case we're looking into can be regarded along these lines. Maybe the women who abducted the two men are just starting out."

"As witches? You think these women have formed some kind of coven?" Katy folded her arms and perched her backside on one of the desks near the board.

"I don't know. It's all supposition at this point and all we have to go on. AJ, any further news on the vehicles?"

"No, I looked through every CCTV camera angle and still couldn't find a plate number before the cars headed out into the country."

Karen Titchard cleared her throat and raised a hand to speak. "Go on, Karen. Just shout it out." Lorne smiled encouragingly at the young detective constable.

"I've been thinking about this at home. If we've got little to go on, we need to remember that these crimes were committed within striking distance of each other."

"Yes, go on," Katy prompted her.

Karen went to her computer screen, tapped the keyboard, and turned the screen to face the crowd. She circled an area on the map with her finger. "This area here. If the cars were seen heading out into the country, I think this is the only possible route they could have taken."

"All right if I interrupt there?" AJ asked.

Katy nodded.

"We know in what direction the cars went after leaving town, so I don't understand what you're getting at, Karen."

"Just a sec, AJ. My line of thinking is this—we should be on the lookout for a dwelling along this route, not too far out of town. Maybe we can do a search for places, like farms for instance, with outbuildings on the land."

Katy's eyes narrowed as she thought. "Lorne, didn't you say that Carol mentioned a cave or stone walls? Or did I imagine that?"

"You're right."

"A cellar of sorts, perhaps?" Karen offered. "I could ask a friend of mine in the planning department if he knows of anything like that situated in this or the surrounding area."

"Yep, do that, Karen, and get back to us. I think we should all search the Internet to see what else we can discover about modern-day witchcraft. Lorne, do you want to ring Carol, see if she can offer anything?"

"Good idea. I'll get on it right away."

"Anything else, folks?" Katy asked, launching herself off the desk. When there was no response, she dismissed the crowd and returned to her office.

"Carol, it's Lorne. How are you?"

"Excited. I told Ted, and he said he'd be willing to lend a hand with any maintenance needed around the centre once Tony's business takes off."

"Wow, really? That'll be a load off everyone's mind. I'm sure Tony wasn't looking forward to working around the centre at the weekends. Not that being a PI is a Monday-to-Friday kind of job. Not sure he's grasped that concept, either." Lorne chuckled.

"He'll be fine. I doubt his MI6 days consisted of a nine-to-five schedule, five days a week, either. What can I do for you? I'm guessing this call is about your case?"

"Yep, something you picked up on yesterday—Pendle."

"I remember. What about it?"

"You didn't make the link yourself to Pendle Hill?"

Carol gasped. "Goodness me! The thought never even crossed my mind. How absurd. You think there are witches involved in these crimes?"

"I'm going along those lines, yes. I might end up with egg on my face, but I think we should be following what you picked up on. You've never let us down in the past, and we've got very little else to chase at this time. Anyway, Katy told me to ring you to see if you had any idea of any of these sorts of shenanigans going on in our area."

"I've not heard of anything on the circuit. I'm sure I would've done if there had been. Psychics like to gossip, just like anyone else. I could make a few calls for you, if you like? Maybe there's a group of women just pretending to be witches or just setting out. Gosh, I'm beginning to sound like you, throwing up all sorts of possible solutions."

Lorne snorted. "I just wish our roles were reversed sometimes and that I had your abilities. It would make my life a whole lot better. Please do ring around your friends. It'll be interesting to see what you can find out. I'll speak later. Thanks, Carol, and thank Ted for me, too."

"I will. I'll get back to you as soon as I find anything out."

Lorne hung up and called home. The phone rang and rang, but neither Tony nor Charlie picked up. She thumped the side of her head when she remembered that Charlie had a home visit booked that morning, and Tony had hinted he wanted to take a trip into town to pick up supplies for the centre. She made a mental note to ring back later. She had more research to carry out regarding witchcraft. *How does someone even become a witch? Is there a society they join? Magicians have the Magic Circle. Do witches need to belong to something similar? Or can a coven start up out of the blue?*

She soon discovered that lots of different types of witches practised the craft in its varying forms in the UK. She hadn't realised it was so prevalent. Most of the covens practised Pagan rituals, inoffensive and erring on the side of nature. However, Lorne did uncover something very disturbing. Way back in the sixties, several covens had formed and caused havoc in a few rural communities. They had all pretended to be good witches, the pagan sort, when they first started practising the craft. However, something went drastically wrong, turning them into bad witches who carried out unspeakable things to victims, even murdering some of the men who were commissioned to hunt them down. In the New Forest, several men's bodies had been found hanging from the trees. Suspicion had lain at the witches' doors, yet authorities had failed to find any proof of wrongdoing on their part. In the end, the coroner had registered the men's deaths as suspected suicides. *Maybe someone in this group of women is keen to emulate either the Pendle Witches or the witches who went bad in the New Forest?*

Lorne didn't know how they were going to locate this coven in a timely manner. If the missing men had fallen into the hands of women of this ilk, intent on copying the witches from years ago, then these men's lives wouldn't be worth living within a few days, if they were still alive.

CHAPTER ELEVEN

Felicity and the four women who'd drawn the short straws to accompany her on the mission, drove to the car rental place to pick up the van for the day's outing.

Elaine, Sally, Mary, and Lenora all looked nervous as they loaded into the van. Felicity had spent hours running through the plan in her head, and the time had come to put that plan into action. Each woman had eventually volunteered her ex-partner to be abducted next. The first man on the list was Elaine's ex, Lee Carney. He worked for a local mechanic.

"Are you ready, Elaine? You know what to do, right?"

"Yes, although I'm very nervous. He tends to fly off the handle at a moment's notice, especially when he's disturbed at work. I just hope he falls for the line I'm going to feed him."

"Just remember to smile, flutter your eyelashes a lot, and sweet charm him into following you out to the van. We'll take things from there. All right, hon?"

"Yes. Okay. I'm going now, before my nerve abandons me." Elaine hopped out of the van and approached the main entrance of the garage workshop.

"How are things back there? Are you all tooled up? Be ready—we'll hit him quick, before he has a chance to figure out what we're up to. Let's hope Elaine can pull this off."

The women said they were geared up and ready for action, and Felicity ducked down in her seat then peered over the edge of the steering wheel. "Here we go, girls," she said when she saw Elaine and Lee coming their way. "Once the sliding door at the side opens, I want you to hit him and drag him into the van."

"It's just in here." Elaine was outside her window, so Felicity sank lower in her seat.

"What the...? Why have you got this huge van? Have you hired it? You can't drive a beast like this."

"I can. I have done a lot of things since our divorce, Lee. I just need you to take a look at this."

The van door slid back, and from her cramped position, Felicity saw Lee poke his head in the rear. He started to object, then a metal pole connected with his skull. The man's heavy body slumped. Three sets of arms grabbed wherever they could reach while Elaine pushed his rump with all her might. With suppressed cheers and fists clenched in triumph, they rejoiced in their success.

"Elaine, shut the door and get in. We need to get out of here quickly."

The woman seemed glued to the spot.

Felicity stretched across the passenger's seat and shoved open the door. It stopped inches from the stunned woman's face. "Elaine? Now!"

Elaine shook her head, slammed the side door shut, and hoisted herself into the front seat, next to Felicity. "Sorry, I just can't believe we pulled it off. Let's go before his boss comes back."

"You've got it." Felicity patted Elaine's thigh. "Well done, you. Right, if he's all trussed up, we'll be on our way. Who's next? Sally, your ex works near here, didn't you say back at the house?"

The inoffensive woman nodded and gulped. "Yes, he works in a factory, as a shop floor manager."

"Okay, do you think it will be possible for you to entice him out into the car park the same way Elaine just did?"

"I think so. I can use my son as an excuse to see him. He ignores any contact from me unless it is about one of the children," she said, seeming to gain confidence once she'd thought up the excuse.

"Excellent, and shame on him ignoring you. Still, you can get your revenge later for all the heartbreak he's put you through over the past year."

Sally smiled and nodded. "Don't worry. I'd already thought of that. I'm really looking forward to exacting my revenge. Take the first road on the right. That's a shortcut to the factory."

"Great. Let's go and pick up another target. I'm beginning to enjoy this. Aren't you, girls?"

A large cheer rang out from the back of the van. Elaine, however, said nothing. Felicity winked at her friend. "Are you having fun, Elaine?"

"Sorry, I was miles away. Just thinking how much fun I'm going to have later getting my own back on the bastard I wasted so many years on."

"That's the spirit, love. Onwards!"

Sally hopped out of the van in the road adjacent to the factory car park. Felicity thought that would be best, given the way Lee had reacted upon seeing the van his ex-wife had pulled up in.

Within minutes, Sally reappeared with a tall, handsome man in tow. She led her ex to the side door. The second the metal door slid back and Terry popped his head in, one of the girls struck him. A surprised "humph" filled the van as he hit the deck. Sally struggled to push him in, and with only two girls in the back to pull the dead weight, the whole process took longer than anyone had anticipated. Felicity jumped out and heaved Sally's ex into the van. Sally crawled in beside him and proceeded to tie his wrists together.

Hopping into the driver's seat once more, Felicity asked who was next on the list. Lenora said it was her ex's turn to take the hit. Paul Dollins was a chef in a pub on the edge of town. If any of the targets were going to be tricky, it was this one.

"If you go round the back, I'm sure we'll be able to get away with this without anyone seeing us." Lenora motioned to where Felicity should park.

"One thought just hit me, Lenora. Will he be at work at this time of day, mid-afternoon? Isn't that between shifts for a chef working in a pub?"

"Nope, Paul is very dedicated to his work. That's the main reason why our marriage failed. He was tired most of the time, and that irritability led to him abusing me. Let me see if I can be as successful as Elaine and Sally."

Lenora walked briskly through the rear entrance of the pub and re-emerged soon after with her angry-looking ex stomping behind her like a petulant child.

"This one looks as though he might be trouble, girls. Be prepared to whack him hard a few times if necessary," Felicity said.

Lenora grimaced, no doubt knowing that Felicity was watching, awaiting their arrival. The side door slid back.

"What the fuck is going on here? Where's Jake?" Paul asked.

Whack! Whack! Silence was followed by the grunts of four women heaving the unconscious man into the van.

"Lenora, tie him up. Well done. I know it wasn't easy. He seems a right idiot. I might even give you a hand dishing out the punishment later, if you'll permit me? Okay, one more pick up, and then we'll get back to the cottage. Mary, you've seen what's expected. Are you up to the task?"

Mary snorted. "I'm looking forward to it. Bring it on, I say." The woman in her early fifties eagerly rubbed her hands together.

The van's occupants erupted with laughter as Felicity drove away from the pub. One of the men stirred, and Felicity gave permission to knock him out with a second blow.

Mary's ex worked in a furniture store on the large trading estate. Like the others, she went inside to retrieve her ex. This man, who was short, looked like a puppy dog, eager to please, as he followed Mary to the van. His chin nearly slammed into the ground when he saw the other women and the three unconscious men in the rear of the van. Before he could open his mouth to complain, Mary shoved him in the back, and Lenora smacked him around the head with the metal pole.

"Impossible mission now completed in record time, ladies. Job well done. Now let's get going and start having some fun."

* * *

Lorne was on her way home from work when her mobile rang. She placed the phone in the hands-free slot. "Hello. This is Lorne."

"Lorne, it's John back at the station. We've received an urgent call from a man claiming to be your neighbour."

Her heart flipped several times before she finally found her voice. "Go on, John."

"Apparently, he's seen some of your dogs out on the road. He's tried to round a few up, but gave up and decided to ring you instead."

"Oh, shit! Where's my husband and daughter? Did he say?"

"He said he'd knocked on the door to the house and received no answer. I'm sorry, Lorne."

"Thanks, John. I'm nearly there now."

Lorne hung up and pressed her foot to the floor. She arrived at the house within five minutes, to find scared dogs milling about the main road and her driveway. Beckoning a black lab, she hooked her hand through his collar and led him back into the kennel block, only to find that the kennels looked as though they had been opened deliberately.

Where the heck are Charlie and Tony? She called out for them and quickly checked the house, which was empty. *Oh my God, what if something has happened to them?* The screech of brakes on the main road tore her from her indecision over what to do next. If she didn't round up the rest of the dogs, they would cause a car accident while intent on enjoying their freedom.

After locking up another escapee, she heard a car draw up. She ran outside, hoping to see her husband or daughter. Instead, Carol stood in the driveway, looking as distraught as Lorne felt.

"Thank God you're here, Carol. Help me get them back in the kennels, please?"

"Damn, I'm sorry, Lorne. It was him, Onyx's owner. By the time the vision formed fully, it was too late to warn you."

"We can't worry about that now, Carol. Where the hell are Charlie and Tony? They should be here." Her thoughts cleared, she slammed her clenched fists against her thighs, angry at herself. "What am I thinking? What if he's harmed them in some way? My God, what if he's raped Charlie?"

Carol grabbed Lorne's upper arms and shook her. "Stop it! Don't even consider *that*, Lorne. I'm sure he hasn't harmed them. Let's sort the dogs out for now."

"If you're sure they're all right, let's try and coax the dogs around here inside while I head out to the road. I'm more concerned about those out there being struck by passing vehicles. Grab some food from the barrel, shake it in the metal bowl. They should respond to that."

"Righty-o. Don't fret, love. We'll get them all."

Tony's car arrived, and Lorne stomped across the gravel to meet him. She yanked open the door and shouted, "Where the hell have you been?"

Tony looked up at her, confusion swimming in his eyes. "What's going on? Why are the dogs out on the road?"

"I haven't got time to explain. Help me and Carol to get them back inside."

Tony leapt from the car and ran out onto the main road. He reappeared with two of the smaller dogs and handed them to Carol.

Almost an hour later, most of the kennels were full again. Charlie's car pulled into the drive about the same time Lorne realised that Onyx and her pups were missing.

"Mum? Everything all right? You look stressed."

"Stressed! That's a severe understatement. Where have you been, Charlie?"

Charlie frowned, and her back straightened. Lorne prepared herself for an argument.

"Out! You know I had a home visit to attend to. What's with the questions?"

"Someone opened all the kennels. Carol and I have spent the last hour rounding the dogs up," Lorne snapped back.

"Shit. I can totally understand you being narked at me, Mum, but I thought Tony would be here. The home visit was so close to Melinda's house, I dropped in to see her. I'm so sorry."

"Well, he wasn't here. I've yet to get to the bottom of that, but I think you've both been selfish and irresponsible. Now, Onyx and her pups are missing. Carol seems to think her owner has taken her and released all the dogs out of spite."

"We have to call the police then."

"I *am* the police, in case you have forgotten, Charlie."

"Yeah, all right. There's no need to be sarcastic, Mum."

Tony joined them, his expression sheepish, when he overheard their conversation. "I hold my hands up, ready to take the blame on this one. I went out for supplies and bumped into one of my old agent friends. We got chatting, and I lost track of time. The good news is that Joe is interested in setting up a business with me."

Lorne issued him a dirty look. "Mind if we discuss this when we have more time? I have a kennel full of scared dogs to placate and feed and an incident of dog-knapping to report."

"I understand. Stupid of me not to realise the gravity of the situation. What can I do to help?"

Lorne expelled a long breath. "You can stay out of my way for now. That would help no end."

Tony took a step back. Everyone in their right mind knew to shut up and just do as they were told when Lorne was so angry. She ran into the house and made two calls. She contacted the station to report the theft and ask them to prioritise the call for Onyx's sake. The other call was to the RSPCA inspector dealing with the dog's case.

"Hi, Sue. It's Lorne Warner. We have a serious problem."

"I'm all ears. Is this concerning the little mummy dog?"

"Yes. Someone broke in, sort of, while we were away and let all the dogs out. I came home to find every boarder and permanent resident wandering the nearby area."

"My God, Lorne, that's horrendous. Who would do such a thing?"

"I'm guessing it's Onyx owner. When I looked in her kennel, she and her pups were missing. Even her bed had disappeared. None of the other kennels had been emptied like that."

"Okay, it seems strange asking a copper this, but have you informed your lot?" Sue asked, concern evident in her voice.

"That's the first call I made. I wanted to ask your opinion, really—if anybody has stolen back a dog, where do they likely take it? He wouldn't be stupid enough to take it back to his home address, surely?"

"It's not unheard of, Lorne, although most of the time, they tend to find an empty shed at a friend's or a neighbour's house and store the animal there until all the fuss has died down."

Lorne began pacing the lounge. "Oh, crap! Do you think we'll ever find Onyx?"

"I have no idea. Sometimes we manage to find the animals before it's too late, and others, we don't. I've got a phone number for one of his neighbours here. Let me give the lady a call and get back to you. All right?"

"That's great, Sue. I'll be waiting for your call."

Lorne hung up and threw the phone at the sofa. "Shit!"

She flinched when Tony's arms wrapped around her.

He pulled back a little and turned her to face him. "I'm so sorry, love. What more can I say or do?"

"I know, I'm sorry for having a go at you, too. What's done is done. There's no point being angry at each other. That won't bring Onyx back, will it?"

"Thanks for being so understanding, love. I'm sorry Charlie and I let you down."

"Let's hope we can find the poor dog and her pups soon. I'm waiting for Sue to call back, then we'll need to sit down and put a plan into action. I think I'll give Katy a call and see if I can get the day off tomorrow. I'm not going to stop searching until I find Onyx, especially after what Sue just said. I have a feeling this Metcalfe will lock Onyx up somewhere and throw away the key. Maybe, if we give her some time, Carol will conjure up a vision that'll lead us to her. I just hope he hasn't harmed those pups. We found them tied up in a black bag, remember?"

"Ring Katy. I think we need to pull out all the stops to find Onyx. If we throw enough resources at the hunt, we should succeed soon."

Lorne picked up the phone again and rang Katy's mobile. "Hi, hon. Sorry to disturb you at home, but I have some bad news and need a favour."

"What's wrong? Is it Tony?"

"No. We've been broken into, I suppose you'd call it. We think Onyx's owner, this Metcalfe guy, has taken her and the pups. I came home to find them missing and all the other kennels wide open."

"What? All the dogs were set loose? Is the place usually left unattended during the day?"

"Sore point. Both Tony and Charlie had appointments. I was wondering if I could take the day off tomorrow?"

"Sure, I don't see why not. Things are a little quiet at the station with the case now anyway. Just the day, though, okay?"

"You have my word. We're all going to start searching for Onyx now. The RSPCA are aware and keeping an eye open. Carol is here, too. We're hoping she'll be able to come up with some clues soon. Other than that, I think it's going to be a case of trawling the streets."

"Have you rung the station and reported Onyx as stolen?"

"Yes, it was my first call."

"What about this Metcalfe guy? Did you run his name through the system? We could put an alert out for his car if he has one."

"No, I didn't get the chance to do that. Would Roberts be upset if I did that, do you think? Using the police searches for personal access goes against the rules, doesn't it?"

"Not when a crime has been committed, Lorne."

"You're right. Okay, I'll get back on to the station and see what I can find out. Thanks, Katy. You're a star."

"Ring me anytime. Keep me informed, and good luck. Try and restrain yourself when you finally catch up with the bastard, all right?"

"I'll try. Ring you tomorrow with a progress report."

"Good luck."

Lorne ended the call, and the phone rang in her hand before she could put it down again. "Hello? Lorne Warner."

"Lorne, it's Sue at the RSPCA. I managed to contact the neighbour, and she said she saw Metcalfe leave the property mid-afternoon. Unfortunately, she hasn't seen or heard him since he left. I'll get the inspectors to keep an eye out in the area. Apart from that, there is little else we can do at this end."

"Okay, Sue. I'm taking the day off work tomorrow to start a thorough search. Do you think he'll use somewhere near his home?"

"That's usually the case, Lorne. I wish I could be more help."

"You've been brilliant so far, Sue. I'm going to ring the station back to see if I can track down his vehicle registration number. I'll ask our lot to keep their eyes peeled for his car. Maybe between us, we'll find him. Be in touch soon."

"Okay, sounds good. I'll call you the second I hear anything."

Lorne rang the station and asked the duty desk sergeant to look into Metcalfe's details and put out an alert. He was all too happy to oblige and also wished Lorne luck in her search. Then both she and Tony walked into the kitchen to find Carol and a subdued Charlie waiting for them.

"Anything?" Carol asked as she grasped Charlie's hand tighter.

"Nothing as yet. I'm taking the day off work tomorrow."

Charlie's red, swollen eyes latched on to hers.

"Mistakes happen in life, Charlie. You should know that better than anyone, love. It'll be all right. I'm confident we'll find Onyx. We have the best detective team on the case, after all. Both Tony and I will be out there searching for her."

"That's great, Mum. Is there anything I can do?"

"Stay here and look after the other dogs. I need to organise some form of security gate at the main road entrance. Maybe we should have thought of that sooner. I never even imagined someone would attempt to steal the dogs from under our noses. I should've known better."

"I'll have a word with Ted, if you like? See if he has any contacts in the trade."

"That'll be great, Carol. One less job to think about. Thanks. Can you keep asking the spirit world? See if anything comes through there?"

"I keep asking, but there's very little coming my way. I'll keep trying."

"Great. Here's the plan if everyone is agreeable. I'll knock up some quick omelettes—we'll need some sustenance before we begin. I suspect we have a long night ahead of us. Then Tony and I will set off to start the search around Metcalfe's house. I fear the worst for Onyx, but I have to give it my best shot to find the poor dog and her pups."

"I'll lend a hand with the cooking," Carol offered, "then try and find a quiet spot to tune in to my spirit guides."

Lorne hated being reliant on Carol's contacts. However, she sensed this was the only real answer to their problem.

CHAPTER TWELVE

Felicity beamed as she surveyed the group of men in front of her, each either confined to the stocks or chained to the wall. Some of the men were still unconscious, and it was time to bring them round. Each woman whose former partner had been captured had filled a bucket with cold water and was standing within inches of her ex.

"On my command, let them have it, ladies. One, two, three, and go!"

Four buckets of water hit their targets in unison, and four men gasped for air, wondering what kind of hell they had woken up to. They glanced around the room and down at their naked bodies then tried to twist out of their confines.

"Waste of time, gents. There's no one escaping these beauties. Just relax and take what's coming to you like brave little soldiers, okay?" Felicity said.

Jordan's laughter filled the room. He grimaced as if remembering the pain filling his mouth. "Best you keep your mouths shut, guys. They stripped me of all my teeth. I sense they're about to make your lives not worth living. I hope you have the ability and courage to overcome what is heading your way." He nodded in David's direction and said bitterly, "He's been lucky so far, kept his mouth shut. That's the key."

Felicity applauded his outburst. "He's right, boys. Keep your mouths shut, and you'll be let off lightly. Start dishing out the same sort of crap you used to give your partners, and we've got all manner of torture techniques lined up for you. Now, what's it going to be?"

Silence filled the cavernous room until Felicity prodded the first man in line, Lee, in the side with the pointed poker.

"Ouch, you bitches won't get away with this. I ain't bothered what you do to me. I'm not sure what you're after, but I ain't going to start licking your feet or doing anything as disgusting as that. Nothing you do to me will make me regret the way I treated Elaine. Nothing," Lee roared.

In spite of the new man speaking out, she decided to inflict more pain on Jordan. The man had annoyed her that much she felt the more suffering he incurred would help keep the others in line. "Let's see about that, shall we? Obviously, Big Mouth over there hasn't learned to keep his trap shut yet, so watch and learn, men. Watch and learn." Felicity dipped behind the curtain off to her left and returned carrying a blowtorch. She had no idea what kind of damage it could do, but she was intent on finding out. The fear in Jordan's eyes made her want to laugh out loud. Instead, she kept her face straight and full of menace. She walked past the row of newly acquired victims, amidst gasps and murmurings, and halted in front of her challenger.

"You wouldn't dare. You could kill me with that. If you can make it work, that is. I'll be better off to you alive. I'm no good to you dead, dear lady. I have money," he added, his voice shaking.

Felicity hitched up one of her shoulders and taunted him. "With all these other volunteers available, who cares if it goes wrong, Jordan."

His eyes bulged. He continued to watch her tamper with the control and leaned back when the flame emerged from the spout of the tool. She waited a second or two, sensing the tension mounting from all quarters of the room, before she motioned for Dara to flick the light switch. Dara hesitated. Felicity urged her to get on with it, but Dara dithered too long for Felicity's liking.

"Julie, do the honours please?"

Julie turned off the lights. Everyone's focus turned to Jordan. He cried out as the flame came nearer, his gaze fixated on the blue hues within its depths. He squirmed more as the heat got closer to the hairs on his chest. Then he started thrashing around when his hairs frizzled under the heat. Then his skin turned scarlet before it wrinkled under the intensity of the heat. His face contorted and he screamed, he blinked wildly as his naked body was overcome by more pain than any human being could bear for more than a few seconds.

Felicity withdrew the flame and raised her hand for Julie to turn on the light switch again. She narrowed her eyes, daring the barely conscious man to challenge her further. Then he startled her by summoning the strength for one last venomous onslaught.

"You'll never break me, no matter how hard you try. You think you have this all worked out, don't you, *leader?*"

"Your insubordination will be the death of you, Jordan. I'd watch my mouth if I were in your position," Felicity warned, thinking up an extra-special technique to wipe the grin from his face once and for all. Something sparked at the back of her mind. She would need to think things through before attempting to carry out the wacky scheme, and the idea was sure to put a strain on the group if she voiced it openly. As for Dara, she knew the woman wouldn't agree to such an ambitious plan, but Felicity would go through with it, nevertheless. She was in charge, after all. At least Jordan had cottoned on to that fact.

Anyone who objected to what she had in mind for this man could leave. They knew where the door was. Felicity placed a finger under Jordan's chin, angling his head up to look at her.

"Don't push me too far. I promise you'll regret it."

The man's lip curled, then he turned his head to the side, unhooking it from her finger, and spat on the floor in front of Felicity. "Bring it on, lady. Do your worst. You've got neither the guts nor the intelligence to get the better of me."

"We'll see. For now, you'll keep. I'll use and abuse you because it suits me to do that right now. However, one day, I will teach you a lesson neither of us will forget."

He tilted his head back and let out a long, deranged laugh that would have curdled any nearby milk.

Seething, Felicity worked her way back up the line of men, prodding each one she passed with the poker. She took pleasure in ignoring their cries of pain. She blanked out the noise, intent on working through the mechanics of her new plan. She called the women into the next room and closed the door.

"This is what we're going to do—I want you each to tell me what these men have stripped you of. Name three things that you're eager for them to return, either materialistic or emotional things. Then we're going to torture each one until he surrenders the items. I think some will relinquish the material items quickly, whereas others, such as Jordan, will require further encouragement. Let me have the three things before tomorrow, and over the weekend, I'll create a legal document that each of the men will sign. If they refuse, then they'll suffer.

"Ladies, we need to get back to our normal lives and routines. Therefore, I suggest we all go home for the weekend. I'll return periodically to feed and water the men, but it will also do them good to think we have deserted them. Does anyone have a fierce-looking dog they are willing to lend us for a week or so?"

The group shook their heads.

"Never mind. I'm sure I can come up with a solution for that."

"I saw something on the TV the other night about a local rescue centre being inundated with dogs at the moment. You could give them a call or drop by and see if they have any suitable dogs," Mags offered from the back of the group.

"Good thinking. I'll look them up and call in to see them tomorrow. In the meantime, we keep subjecting the men to small bouts of discomfort. Any lip from any of them, you must promise me that you'll dish out the necessary punishment, okay?"

The women all agreed.

"Very well. Don't forget to give me your lists, and I'll get to work on the finer details over the weekend. I also want to look up some possible spells we can use to help guide the men to make the right choices, should they have any doubts."

"Spells? What kind of spells?" Julie asked, frowning.

"I haven't quite worked out that side of things yet. That's why I need to have a break over the weekend. Do you know where the special spell book is offhand?"

"I think so. Leave it with me. Do you need a hand organising anything? I'm free over the weekend."

"Thank you, Julie. Let's see what happens tomorrow with regards to the rescue centre and go from there."

* * *

Defeated, after going door-to-door, Lorne and Tony returned empty-handed from their search for Onyx and her pups.

"Maybe tomorrow will bring better news, love," Tony said.

Tony's attempt to keep her spirits up worked for a few minutes, until an image seeped into her mind: Onyx lying in a cold, dark place, trying to protect her pups. Tears pricked her eyes. Tony gathered her in his arms, and she could do nothing else but break down and cry.

"Why? How could he do this to her? He discarded her once. It's as if he's saying 'screw you, lady. She deserves to die.'"

"I know, love. Let's try and get some rest, and then we'll both get out there again first thing. We'll find her. I promise you that."

"I hope so, Tony. I have severe doubts on this one." Lorne pushed away from him. He wiped the tears from her cheeks and kissed her on the nose. "I'm going to check in with the station. Can you make us a coffee please?"

"Will do. I'll just pop upstairs to see how Charlie is doing first."

"Oh, crap! No, I should have thought of doing that as soon as we got home. I'll go." Lorne ran upstairs to find Charlie sitting crossed-legged on her bed with her iPod playing.

"Mum, any news on Onyx?"

Lorne collapsed on the bed beside her daughter and stroked her arm. "No, love. I take it there have been no calls while we were out?"

"Nothing. I've been sitting here, thinking what we can do, and I keep coming up blank, except for one idea I keep returning to."

"What's that, sweetie?"

"Call the TV station again, ask if they'll help find her."

Lorne smiled proudly. "I had that same thought then changed my mind."

"Why?"

"I think this Metcalfe will be hoping we do something along those lines. He'll just sit there, laughing at us. You can be assured that he's got her tucked away in a secure place out of sight of people."

"Oh, Mum. What if he's already killed her and the pups? Are we to blame for parading Onyx on TV? Is that how these warped-minded people work?"

"It's a hard lesson to learn, love, one that I'm not keen on repeating in the future. People who abuse animals are the scum of the earth. It really never occurred to me that they would be devious, too. I guess nothing should surprise me nowadays. Do you want to come downstairs and sit with us for a while? It's not good to stew things over up here alone."

"I'm going to bed soon, Mum."

"Okay, shall I fetch you up a drink of cocoa?"

Charlie smiled. "Just like you used to do at the weekends when I was a kid, you mean."

That one tiny off-the-cuff comment stabbed Lorne in the chest. She'd only ever been around to make a fuss of her daughter at the weekend because of work. She told herself she was being silly and that Charlie was turning into a remarkable young woman, despite the mishap that had happened today. She still wouldn't swap her daughter for most of the teens running around, causing havoc on the streets of London.

"Yes or no?" she asked with a wink.

"Cocoa would be nice. Thanks, Mum."

Lorne stood up and leaned over to kiss her daughter on the forehead. "I love you, sweetheart. Keep strong. We'll get Onyx and her family back soon."

"I love you too, Mum. Let's hope so."

Lorne returned to the kitchen, turned on the kettle, then bent down to cuddle Henry. "I'm so glad you were in the house today, boy. If you'd got out, I would have been beside myself. I'd be lost without my little buddy hanging around."

Henry licked her face then rested his chin on her shoulder, sensing her need for a cuddle from her best mate.

Tony joined them, sporting a sympathetic smile on his face. "Good job he didn't get let out today, eh?"

"I just had that conversation with him. Do you think he would have run off?"

"Nah, he knows when he's on to a good thing. He'd be just as lost without you as you would be without him. I'll make the drinks. Coffees all round, is it?"

"Nope, Charlie wants one of her mum's special cups of cocoa."

"Oh, right. Well, I better leave that to you then. How about ringing the station, see if they've got any news on Metcalfe?"

"You read my mind." Lorne kissed Henry then made her way into the lounge to use the phone. "Hi, it's Lorne Warner. Any news for me?"

"I was in the process of chasing that up for you, ma'am. Hold the line." Lorne tapped her foot while she waited for the desk sergeant to return. "I'm back. Right, we've had a sighting of his vehicle down by the river in Guildford, about twenty minutes from his home."

"That's strange. Has anyone investigated the area?"

"No, not yet, ma'am. The team which called it in caught a glimpse of the car while attending another crime scene. I'm sorry it's not better news for you."

"It's a start. I'll just note down the location, and Tony and I will take a gander tomorrow."

The desk sergeant told her the address, and she hung up. Lorne waved the piece of paper as she re-entered the kitchen. "We just might have a new area to search tomorrow or…"

Tony shook his head in despair. "Like that's going to wait until tomorrow. Is it far?"

Lorne sniggered. "We'll have our drinks and take a drive out there. It's about thirty minutes from here."

Tony volunteered to drive as Lorne was too wound up. "Down here, according to the map."

"If he's still at the scene, let me handle it, okay? There's no telling what stunt the idiot will try to pull off."

"Yes, boss," Lorne agreed.

Tony cut the engine, and the car glided to a halt near the river. Looking around, Lorne saw several possible hiding places. Thankfully, the area seemed clear of any sign of Metcalfe, and the likelihood of him returning at this hour seemed remote.

"You take that side, and I'll start from that end. We'll meet in the middle. Make sure you listen carefully. If you scratch the door, the pups will probably start to whimper. Any noise, call me straight away."

"Yes, dear." Tony shook his head and marched off to the far end of the row of garden sheds. Lorne suspected they were in some kind of allotment. Metcalfe would have been careless to leave the dogs in such a place, given the frequency folks visited the garden patches.

Lorne scratched the door of the first shed and used her torch to peer through the window, but heard and saw nothing of interest, so she moved on to the next one and received the same negative result. She looked up to see Tony waving frantically at her. She ran at full speed to reach him. "Is she in there?"

"It certainly sounds like it to me. Listen." He stepped back so that she could place her ear to the slight crack in the door.

"Me, too. Oh, Tony, we've found her."

"That's a pretty hefty lock on the door. Let me see what tools I have in the back of the car." Tony hobbled back to the car, favouring his prosthetic leg. He returned a few moments later with a set of bolt cutters. "I picked them up a few months back at the market. We'll soon find out how good they are. Stand back."

"What the fuck do you think you're doing, arsehole?" a voice boomed out behind them, its owner hidden by the darkness.

Tony turned and raised the bolt cutters above his head, ready to retaliate if the man attacked him.

"You should have known you wouldn't get away with this, Metcalfe. Open the door and return the dogs to us, or I'll arrest you on the spot."

"Ha, arrest me, my arse. Who the fuck do you think you are, wannabe heroes?"

"You're an idiot. You've messed with the wrong people." Lorne reached into her jacket pocket and showed him her warrant card. "DS Warner, at your service. You're nicked."

The man turned and took off in his best impression of Usain Bolt running in one of his world-record-setting races. Lorne knew Tony would never be able to catch the man if his leg was bothering him, but Tony launched the bolt cutters at Metcalfe's back with all his might, hitting him between the shoulder blades and knocking him off balance. Tony set off and pounced on Metcalfe before he could get to his feet again. Metcalfe threw a left and right hook, but Tony managed to avoid the man's fists. Tony threw one of his own and connected with Metcalfe's chin, sending him reeling backwards. Lorne yanked on the man's hair, and Tony flipped the man over while Lorne slapped on the cuffs. She high-fived Tony.

"Just like old times." Tony laughed and yanked Metcalfe to his feet. He searched the man's pockets and gave Lorne the key to the shed.

Lorne ran to open the shed while Tony placed the man in the back of their car.

"Oh, Onyx, you dear sweet dog. You and your babies are safe." Lorne was upset to see the dog cowering. As Onyx turned away from her, Lorne knew all the progress they'd made over the previous few weeks had gone to pot within hours. Confusion lit the dog's eyes when Lorne gathered her in her arms and placed her gently in the back of the rescue van. Then she returned to the shed to retrieve the dog bed and the four pups, who were still sound asleep. She stroked and kissed them one by one and nestled them beside their mother. Onyx licked the pups' heads and eyed Lorne as she deposited each one. Once the fury family was loaded, Lorne jumped in the passenger seat.

"You won't get away with this. I'm going to do you for assault," Metcalfe shouted from the backseat.

"Yeah, I'd like to see you try. I think the charges against you will far outweigh the one you tag us with, mate. Now, shut up and enjoy your ride to the nick. Hopefully, your last bout of freedom."

CHAPTER THIRTEEN

Lorne still had the following day off work, and she wanted to spend as much time with Onyx as possible so she could regain the dog's trust once again. By mid-afternoon, she had succeeded in sitting next to the dog in the kennel without her flinching every five minutes. Charlie watched her mother deal with the dog, wearing a smile and shedding a few tears of her own. "She's responding finally, Mum."

"She is, love. Compassion and giving her time is all that was needed to make a difference in her life."

"It doesn't cost anything to treat an animal with kindness. If only more people understood that, the world would be a much better place to live in."

Out of the mouths of babes, she thought. *If only all teenagers were as grown-up and caring as Charlie.*

A car drew up outside, and Charlie ran to see who it was. Lorne followed her daughter into the yard as a woman in her early forties stepped out of the car and looked around.

"Hello. Can I help you?" Lorne approached the woman warily.

"Yes, I saw your business advertised on TV the other night and thought I'd drop by to see if you have a dog for me."

"Advertised? Oh, you mean the interview I did regarding Onyx and her pups. We do have a few dogs looking for good homes at the moment. Were you on the lookout for a specific breed?"

Charlie stood alongside Lorne, within nudging distance.

"This is my daughter, Charlie. She actually runs the place."

"How lovely. You're so young, too."

Lorne smiled. "Yes, young but with a very grown-up head on her shoulders. She treats all the dogs the same as if they were our own. If you tell her what you had in mind, she'll do all the necessary paperwork. You are aware that you can't take a dog with you today? We need to carry out a home visit before we let any of our dogs go to new owners. It's our responsibility to make sure the dogs will be cared for properly once they leave here."

"Oh, I see. I was hoping to have a dog by the weekend."

Lorne shook her head. "No can do. Sorry. Was it for a specific reason? Only we don't believe in giving dogs as gifts for birthdays or Christmas presents."

"Oh, no. It was for me. I want it for a guard dog, you see."

"No, I don't, I'm afraid. If you need a dog for a specific reason such as that, then I wouldn't recommend you seek out any rescue dog. They can be very confused creatures. Most of them have come from abusive homes. Therefore, our aim is to restore their faith in humans and ensure they're placed in loving homes, hence the home visits. They're an integral part of the process."

"I see. Well, I won't take up any more of your time in that case."

They all turned as another car pulled into the driveway. Carol got out of her car and joined them. She kissed Lorne then Charlie on the cheek. "Hello. Sorry, am I interrupting something?"

"Not at all. Miss…?"

"Randolph," the woman filled in the blank for Lorne.

"Miss Randolph was after a guard dog." Lorne watched Carol. She'd never witnessed the psychic openly eyeing someone with distaste before. "I'll leave you to bid Miss Randolph farewell, Charlie. Come on, Carol. I have something of interest to show you inside." She linked arms and steered the psychic towards the back door of the house. "What in God's name is wrong with you? Christ, if looks could kill, that woman would be struck down by lightning by now."

"Never, never in all my days as a medium have I felt such a negative energy emanating from someone. Do *not* give that woman a dog, Lorne, ever!"

"What are you picking up, Carol? Maybe I should stick around and see her off the property myself."

"No, she'll be fine with Charlie. There's something evil about her, though, Lorne. Damn, I'm too pumped up to see anything from the spirit guides. Let's have a drink, and I'll try and figure it out."

Carol was trembling. Lorne had never seen her friend so affected by someone's energy before, not someone living, anyway. Tony was sitting at the kitchen table when they went inside.

"Hello, Carol. What do we owe the pleasure?"

"To be honest, I don't know why I'm here." Carol eyed the stranger standing in the courtyard through the kitchen window. "My guess is that it has something to do with your guest, who is now, thankfully, leaving."

"I've never seen you as jumpy as this, Carol. Is she that bad? Is that what you're picking up?"

"I really don't know. Maybe I should've shaken hands with her. I can tell a lot about the vibrations travelling through a person's body."

Lorne ran to the window to see if the woman was still talking to Charlie. "Damn, she's just leaving the drive now."

"I'll go into the lounge. Leave me for a second or two. Let's see what I can come up with."

Lorne joined Tony at the table. She leaned forward and whispered. "That was totally weird. Carol homed in on the woman right away. I've never seen her react like that with anyone, ever. She had a run-in with Pete once, but she still didn't look at him the way she glared at that woman."

"That's strange. And you never picked up anything from the woman. Your people radar is usually shit hot, love."

"Nope, I can't say I did. Maybe my people radar is off kilter with all the hassle going on around here. She seemed nice enough."

"Maybe Carol's wrong about her then."

At that moment, Carol came back into the room, her face drained of colour.

Lorne encouraged her to take a seat. "What on earth is wrong, Carol?"

Carol sat down heavily, placed her head in her hands for a second or two then looked Lorne in the eye. "She's definitely trouble. That won't be the last time you two meet, Lorne. Mark my words on that one."

"Really? In what context? Can you tell me that?"

"Nothing definite as yet, but your paths will cross again in the near future, under very unpleasant circumstances. All I'm picking up is that woman is pure *evil*."

"I'll run a check on her name when I get into work tomorrow."

Suddenly, Carol closed her eyes and began to rock back and forth in her chair. "Jordan."

Lorne frowned and glanced at Tony. Her husband shrugged, and Lorne could tell by the twinkle in his eye that he wanted to respond with a funny retort. She widened her eyes, warning him to keep his mouth shut.

"Stocks. Fingers. Teeth," Carol said.

None of it made sense to Lorne. Experience told her that Carol would keep firing out words, and Lorne would have to piece them all together. She jotted the words on scrap paper, her pen poised ready for more.

"Pain. Men." Carol opened her eyes and flopped back in her chair in exhaustion. "That's it. Make of it what you will, love. All I know is that woman is bad news."

"Thanks, Carol. I'll chase up her details tomorrow and try to make some kind of sense of what you've told me."

"Don't be lax on this one. She's an important player in something that will show up on your radar in the next few days or weeks."

Armed with what Carol had given her about Miss Randolph, Lorne arrived at work to find the other members of her team chattering noisily and looking perplexed.

"Something wrong?"

"Maybe, maybe not," AJ said. "I used my initiative to get in touch with the missing persons hotline, asked them to contact me if any men went missing in a certain area."

"And have they?" Lorne perched on the edge of the nearest desk, the scrap piece of paper from the previous night in her hand.

"Two men. A Lee Carney and Paul Dollins. Both men disappeared the day before yesterday during their shifts at work."

"Did any of their colleagues see anything? Someone hanging around who shouldn't be there, *et cetera*?" Lorne asked.

"Not as far as I can tell. I'm just going to start looking into their backgrounds now. Don't you think it's odd, though? Two men the other day, Jordan and David, and now these two men? If we were looking at cases of women going missing, wouldn't we be treating it as a serial abduction case by now? Just thinking out loud, really," AJ said, booting up his computer.

"I suppose so. Do the usual, AJ—check for CCTV footage." Lorne waved the piece of paper. "I have some checking up of my own to do."

"Oh, what's that about?" Katy came through the outer office door and asked. "Morning, all, by the way."

"We had a strange situation occur at the rescue centre while Carol was there. I'd rather check things out and tell you what I find, if that's okay?"

"Sure. Anything else to report overnight?" Katy walked towards her office.

"We found Onyx and arrested her owner last night, so that's a big relief off our minds. Nasty piece of work, he was. I hope they lock him up and throw away the key."

"Huh, you know that ain't gonna happen, Lorne. I'm glad you found her, though. Poor little mite must have been scared out of her mind. Are the pups all right, too?"

"Yeah, all safe and sound. I'll tell you about the weird experience we had with Carol later. Let me do some research first."

Katy continued walking. "You know where I'll be. You can rescue me anytime you like."

Lorne switched on her computer and did a general search on Felicity Randolph's name. Nothing showed up. She tried a similar search in the vehicle registration files and hit on Felicity Randolph's address. "Jesus!" Lorne scrambled to her feet and marched over to the case notes written on the board.

AJ left his chair and stood beside her. "What is it?"

"I think I've stumbled across a connection to our case. Do me a favour and call Katy."

He took off and returned with their boss in tow.

"What have you found, Lorne?"

"Yesterday, a woman came to the centre looking for a guard dog. I sent her off with a flea in her ear but not before Carol met the woman. Carol picked up on some extremely negative vibes from her. She obtained certain information from the spirits that she expected me to piece together." Lorne waved the piece of paper. "You know how she works, Katy. Anyway, I'll read out what she said slowly and see if you two come to the same conclusion I have. 'Jordan. Men. Pain. Stocks. Fingers. Teeth.'" Lorne glanced at her puzzled-looking colleagues, whose expressions told her they hadn't recognised what she had. "Don't you see? Jordan." Lorne picked up the marker pen and placed a tick by the man's name.

Katy shook her head. "Okay, that much I can make the connection with; as to everything else you've mentioned, I'm sorry, I'm just not connecting the dots. Are you sure you're onto something, Lorne?"

She raised a finger. "Bear with me on this for a second longer. Jordan, men, stocks. Didn't we already speculate that we could be dealing with an S&M issue here?"

"Okay, I'll give you that, even the pain fits your suggestion, but what about teeth and fingers?" Katy asked.

"Let's forget about that side of things for a moment. Here's the interesting part, and I'm sorry for being so slow on the uptake regarding this. It should have occurred to me the second I saw it."

"Now you're talking in riddles. What are you on about?"

"The woman who turned up at my place yesterday—I ran a check on her and came up blank. Then I ran a check on her *car*, and that's when it hit me. AJ, bring up the CCTV footage of the Calleja brothers going off with those women, will you?"

Lorne and Katy followed AJ back to his desk, where he pulled up the file. "That's what I thought. That car and that woman *were* at my bloody property yesterday. Shit! I was so wound up about Onyx that it just didn't register. Holy crap! That Carol picked up such negativity from her just proves her involvement in this."

"All right, Lorne, calm down. Shit happens. How do we rectify the situation? That's what we should be asking."

"Why don't you and I take a ride out to her address?"

Katy surprised Lorne by suggesting, "Let's go. No point in hanging around."

Lorne grabbed her bag and ran after Katy, calling back over her shoulder, "AJ, keep searching that footage. This woman might pop up near the scene. If she does, we've got her."

CHAPTER FOURTEEN

A weird sensation had shadowed Felicity since her visit to the rescue centre. She felt as if someone had stripped her naked, and she struggled to put her finger on why or how. It could have connected with the woman who owned the place or the woman who had arrived at the property just as Felicity was leaving. She concluded that her uneasiness was because of the older woman. She remembered turning to see the woman eyeing her with what appeared to be disdain at one point. At the time, Felicity thought she had imagined it, but the more she recalled the situation, the more certain she became that in the coming few days, their paths would cross again. The next time, there would be a triumphant conqueror. One of them would die.

Julie popped her head around the curtain. "The women are ready. So are the men, for that matter."

"I'll be right there." She shrugged into her black cloak, which empowered her and chased away the sensation causing her angst. Then she collected the gadget she'd picked up on her trip out. She grinned smugly, imagining the men's reaction when they saw it.

Pulling back the curtain, she entered the room. A telling silence descended, interrupted by the odd gasp from one or two of the men.

"Okay, ladies, hand me your lists, if you will?" She walked down the line of women, gathering the sheets of paper each of them held out. Reading through the notes, Felicity sorted them according to how much they disgusted her. The men who deserved the severest treatment went to the back of the pile. "Right, what do we have here? Ladies, when I call your name, please come and stand beside me. Elaine."

With trepidation evident in her stride, Elaine left the group and made her way to join Felicity, who had moved in front of Elaine's ex, Lee.

"Elaine, it says here that your ex-partner failed on many levels. The three things you feel he stole from you the most were your self-respect, your parents' inheritance money, and your love." Felicity turned to the man in question. "So, Lee, tell me—what do you have to say about the charges brought against you? Guilty or not guilty?"

He eyed both of the women as if they had just returned from a stint in an asylum. His lip turned up, and he spat on the ground, missing Felicity's feet by a few inches. "No comment."

Quick as a flash, Felicity aimed the implement she held in her hand and prodded Lee in the chest. The man cried out as the cattle prod made contact with his skin. "Uh, oh! Wrong answer." Felicity withdrew the prod and smiled at Lee. "Do you want to try and answer that question again?" She raised the cattle prod to within inches of his chest, giving him the opportunity to reply before she struck a second time.

"Er... guilty. But there are reasons for that—"

Felicity zapped him again. The man screamed and thrashed around. "Did I ask you to enter into a conversation with me? No. He's guilty, ladies. What do you suggest we do with him?"

The women looked too petrified to speak up, frustrating her more than Lee's response had.

"Come now. Don't be shy. He admitted his guilt. Do we set him free or keep him here?"

A unanimous "keep him" rang out from the crowd. Satisfied with the answer, Felicity continued down the line to the next man.

"Sally, step forward, please?"

Silently, Sally joined Felicity next to her ex. "I'm sorry, Terry," she whispered.

Infuriated, Felicity glared at Sally but said nothing to her friend. She turned to the man trembling in front of them. "Let's see. Well, I'd say Sally here has told some untruths where you're concerned, young man."

"I didn't, I swear," Sally mumbled, her eyes cast down at the ground.

"Let's pick out the worst of his crimes, shall we? Refusing to pay for even the groceries during the seven years you were married." Felicity shook her head in disgust. "You ate the meals she prepared for you, didn't you?"

The man kept quiet.

"How do you think food gets to the table? First, it has to be bought from the shop, packed, carried home, unpacked, and cooked." She spoke to him as though she were explaining the process to a five-year-old.

Finally, the man plucked up enough courage to speak. "I provided her with a roof over her head. I paid all the bills. What more should she have expected?" His voice dripped with sarcasm.

Felicity glanced sideways to see Sally cowering a little when the man spoke. Without warning, Felicity jabbed the cattle prod into Terry's stomach. He yelled, cussing and calling Sally all the names he could think of. Felicity deliberately kept the prod on his skin until he looked as though he would pass out from the pain. Sally ran to his aid, but Felicity yanked her away.

"Mags, Kaz, take Sally out of the room."

The two women marched forward and gently unattached Sally's grasp from her ex's neck.

"I won't leave him. She can't do this—she can't. We have to stop her," she shouted as the two women dragged her into the next room.

Felicity scanned the crowd. "Anyone else going to object before I continue? These men deserve all the punishment they're going to get for the way they've treated you all over the years."

"It's the women who need further punishment from us, not the other way round," the gutsy—or foolish—Jordan shouted.

Felicity stormed over to the insufferable man, yanked his head back, and forced the cattle prod into his mouth. The man shook and twisted violently until Felicity withdrew the tool. "When will you learn to keep your big mouth shut, Jordan? Actually, I've had enough of your outspokenness to last me a lifetime. I have something very special planned for you this evening."

The man's eyes bulged with fear, and the sound of him gulping echoed around the room. "Why? I've done nothing. You have to let me go."

"May I remind you that I don't *have* to do anything! You, on the other hand, are going to suffer for all the pain and anguish you subjected Dara to over the years. I hope to God she now sees the real you. Do you, Dara?"

Dara was near the back of the crowd, hiding behind another of the group members. "Yes," she called out.

"Then believe me when I tell you that your retribution will come to the fore later this evening, dear lady." Turning back to Jordan, she said, "Now keep your trap shut! You hear me?"

A muffled groan escaped his lips. She let go of his hair, and his head dropped onto his chest. The rest of the men accepted their fate and promised to sign over all they had to their ex-partners as recompense for their despicable behaviour. Felicity felt like punching the air when her scheme looked as though it had paid off. Jordan was the only exception. Even his brother, whose wife wasn't even in the group, had agreed he had major faults and had promised to make it up to his wife once Felicity had set him free, *if* she set him free.

CHAPTER FIFTEEN

When Lorne and Katy arrived at Felicity's address, the drive was empty. Suspecting no one was home, Lorne rang the bell just in case.

"Nothing. Shall I go around the back and have nosey?" Lorne asked, already heading towards the alley a few doors up from the terraced house.

"Like I can stop you," Katy called after her. "I'll see if I can spot anything through the window in the meantime."

Lorne entered the back garden easily enough. The piece of string holding the two gates together was hardly a deterrent for intruders. "Some people seriously need to look at their home-security methods," she grumbled.

"Who's there? Get out, or I'll call the coppers," a wizened old man shouted over the fence next door.

Lorne looked over the wooden panel and showed the man her ID. "Hello, sir. I am the police. We're here to speak to Miss Randolph, but she doesn't appear to be at home. Any idea where she might be?"

"How the heck should I know?" he retorted, giving her a puzzled glance.

"Okay, let me ask you this—when was the last time you laid eyes on or heard Miss Randolph at the premises?"

The man played with the sparse whiskers decorating his chin. "Let me think now. Mandy came last Thursday to see me. Was she here then? You know what? I can't remember. It'll be either Wednesday or Thursday of last week."

Disappointed, Lorne wrinkled her nose.

"That's the best I can do, lassie. I don't stand out here all day, keeping an eye on my neighbours, you know."

"I understand. Perhaps you can tell me where she works?"

"Nope. She tends to keep herself to herself, that one. Sorry I can't help you." He started walking towards the back door of his house, obviously fed up with answering her questions.

"Just one last question before you go in, sir. Do you know if she has a boyfriend? Perhaps she's a frequent visitor at his home when she's not here?"

He turned back to her and shrugged. "Wouldn't know, lassie. Like I've said already, she's a bit secretive. Lord knows I've tried to strike up a conversation with her, but she's just not interested. Try Mrs. Connell on the other side. She might know something more."

"Thanks, you've been very helpful. Can I ask you to ring me if she turns up?" She held out a business card for him to collect.

The old man mumbled his annoyance at having to cross the garden again after almost making it into his house. He snatched it from her grasp. "No bother. I'll ring if I can."

Lorne ventured up to Felicity's back door, but it proved pointless. The kitchen was empty, no traces of life at all. *So, if she's not staying here, where is she staying?* Defeated by her exploits, Lorne returned to the front of the house to find Katy already talking to the neighbour on the other side of the suspect's property.

"Any luck?"

Lorne shook her head. "You?"

"No, nothing. Mrs. Connell here seems to think that Felicity is staying somewhere else right now."

Lorne nodded. "I came to the same conclusion after seeing no sign of life around the back. The kitchen is immaculate, not a thing out of place. Have you asked Mrs. Connell when she last saw Felicity?"

"I did. She thinks it was about two weeks ago. She's not certain, though."

"I saw the neighbour who lives next door, and he thought he saw her maybe last Wednesday or Thursday."

Mrs. Connell frowned. "Ah, I was away at my daughter's then, so I couldn't tell you if he's right or wrong."

Katy gave the woman one of her business cards. "Not to worry. Would you mind ringing me if you see her come back here?"

The lady eagerly took the card and tucked it into the pocket of her apron. "I'd be happy to. Can I ask what the urgency to contact her is? It can't be concerning her parents because they died a while back. Poor things, killed outright in a car crash on the motorway."

"Nothing in particular, really. We just want her to help us with our enquiries," Katy replied.

"Ah, I'll be sure to ring you if she shows up. I'm here all day long, apart from when I'm out, of course."

Lorne chuckled as she and Katy made their way back to the car. "That was a touch of the Irish if ever I heard it. What are you thinking?"

Katy unlocked the door, and they both got in. Katy contemplated Lorne's question as she started the car. "Let's get back to the station. Maybe her parents' death could be the key here."

"In what way? A trigger, you mean? The *trigger* which has made her abduct these men, *if* she's abducted them?"

"Maybe. What if her parents had a house somewhere local, and she's staying there instead of at her own home? What if she has reverted back to something grave that took place in her childhood and feels safer at her parents' house rather than here?"

"It's plausible."

"That's the frustrating part."

AJ excitedly beckoned Katy and Lorne over to his desk when they arrived back at the incident room. "I searched all the CCTV footage close to the men's places of work and stumbled across this. I know it's a little late, but at least it's proof that this Felicity Randolph is involved in this crime. I even managed to get a good look at her plate number this time."

"That's great, AJ. We had no luck at her address, unfortunately. Do we know what type of job she does? Maybe we could catch her at work?"

AJ tutted. "I couldn't find anything, not that I really knew where to look. I just carried out a general search. Anyway, I'm glad you're back. I have more disturbing news to add to your woes."

"Well, go on." Katy slumped down in a spare chair. "Add to our frustrating day, why don't you?"

"We're getting reports that another two men have gone missing, both from their workplace. I see a recurring theme here."

"Don't tell me—both in the same area, too?" Katy asked.

"Looks that way, one might be a touch outside the radius we had penned, but it's still within striking distance," AJ confirmed.

"Have you tracked down the CCTV footage yet, AJ?" Lorne asked.

"I'm in the process of doing that now. So far, I've spotted the same car, this Felicity Randolph's car, at one of the scenes. I wonder what her objective is."

"With little else leading us to any possible connections between the men, who's to say what her objectives are? Are the men *just* being abducted, or is there something far more sinister going on? As far as we know, no dead bodies have turned up yet. So the former scenario seems to be the best route to take in our investigation," Lorne told the team thoughtfully.

Just then, DCI Roberts walked into the room. He listened in on their conversation for a moment before he interrupted. "So, let me get this right—we have a prime suspect, yet we can't trace her? I take it all the usual checks have been made to ascertain any other probable addresses where she might be hiding out? Parents, other family members, perhaps?"

Katy clicked her fingers. "We learnt this morning that her parents lost their lives in a car crash. I suppose we could try and locate their home. Maybe they left it to her in their will."

"Good call, Katy. I'll see what I can find out." Lorne hurried over to a spare computer. First, she searched for the couple's death certificates. *Bingo!*

She jotted down the address and returned to the group. "That turned out to be easier than I thought."

"Great job, Lorne." Sean Roberts patted her on the shoulder.

"AJ, can you trace the address on the map and compare it to the direction we spotted Felicity's car going in the other day, on the original CCTV footage when the two brothers were abducted?"

"Give me two secs, and I'll have it." AJ's hands flew across the keyboard.

"Was there anything in particular you wanted, sir?" Katy asked Roberts.

"Not really. I wanted a break from my dreary paperwork duties. I thought I'd amble down here to see how the case was progressing. Is that okay, DI Foster?"

Lorne suppressed the snigger toying with her mouth.

"Oh, yes, fine. If we discover where the address is—it's only a matter of time, knowing AJ's super skills—would you like to venture out there with us, too?" Katy asked her superior.

Lorne waited for the sparks to fly between Katy and Sean Roberts after Katy's sarcastic comment.

However, Sean nodded and waved a finger in the air. "What an excellent idea. It's about time I got out in the field to see how my two favourite women police officers are coping out on the streets."

Katy groaned and headed for her office.

Lorne flicked Sean's arms with her fingers. "You're a wind-up merchant, Sean Roberts."

"That's DCI Roberts, if you don't mind, DS Warner." He grinned and followed Katy into her office.

"I sense trouble," AJ said.

"Nah, Sean—sorry—DCI Roberts is just fooling around. Testing her. God knows I had enough of that treatment from him when I was in Katy's shoes. Come on, let's see what we can find out about this address."

She leaned over AJ's shoulder and watched the screen flip between the tabs he had open at the top. Before long, she felt boggle-eyed and decided to sit down in the chair next to him rather than staring at the constantly changing screen.

"Here it is. I think we're on to something for definite. Shall I put a call in for uniform to go out to the property for a snoop around?"

"Hold off on that for now. I think Katy and I should go out there and see for ourselves first."

Katy's office door opened, and Roberts, looking smug, came out, followed by Katy, who wore a peeved expression.

"Anything?" Roberts asked, obviously adding to Katy's annoyance.

Lorne stifled a grin and concentrated on the screen rather than looking at either of her superiors. "According to the footage from the other day, AJ and I predict the car, or cars, were heading out to this address. Do you want to take a ride out there, Katy?"

"What an excellent idea. Mind if I tag along?" Sean glanced at a furious-looking Katy, who merely shrugged. Then he added, "Of course you don't mind. Shall we go in your car, DI Foster?"

Lorne bit the edge of her mouth, suppressing the giggle dying to escape as Sean continued winding Katy up, making her more and more frustrated by the second.

"Why not?" Katy eventually agreed.

The three of them set off. Katy and Roberts sat up front while Lorne rode in the back. Roberts continually picked fault in either Katy's driving abilities or her intended plan of action once they arrived at the scene. Eventually, Katy hit the roof.

"I'll tell you what, sir. I'm always eager to learn from my superiors, therefore, I suggest that you take charge of this investigation when we reach our final destination. You can show us mere mortals how you professional paper pushers run things out in the field."

Sean Roberts twisted in his seat, his eyes wide and sparkling with amusement.

Lorne shook her head and mouthed, "You asked for that."

He clapped his hands together and laughed. "Bravo, Katy. Now I know that you are made from the same mould as Lorne Warner. I'm only teasing, by the way. I have never, to date, doubted your competency. I insist you take the lead as usual and simply view me as an eager bystander."

"Like that's going to happen," Lorne said, just loud enough for Katy and Sean to hear.

Katy glared at her through the rear-view mirror but said nothing.

"Thanks for that note of sarcasm, DS Warner. You watch, I will step back and let you ladies continue your investigation without my interference," Roberts assured them a second time.

Lorne couldn't help herself—she knew she should have kept quiet. But he'd dangled the carrot, and she couldn't resist taking a large chunk out of it. "How many times have I heard that line over the years?" she mumbled, again loud enough for the others to hear.

They were relatively quiet as they travelled from a built-up urban area out into the wilds of the rural landscape en route to the cottage. After approximately an hour, they stumbled across the cottage by chance more than anything after one of the numerous wrong turns Katy took during the trip.

A fair distance from the house, Katy parked the car, then the three of them set off towards the cottage, scanning the area around them for any sign of life.

"Let's hope we don't regret not organising an armed response team as backup," Lorne said when they reached the edge of the front garden.

"No need to panic just yet," Katy replied then whispered, "How do you want to play this? Should we knock on the door and announce ourselves or just snoop around for now?"

Sean glanced at Lorne for a response. "Gee, thanks! I think we should snoop for now. There are no vehicles here at the moment. That's not to say there isn't one parked around the back or in a barn somewhere. I'll take the rear."

"Good idea. What do you want to do, DCI Roberts?" Katy asked, still looking uncertain about Sean's role out in the field.

"You tell me what you want me to do, DI Foster. This is your baby."

Lorne shook her head. "Guys, sort it out and cut the crap, for God's sake. People's lives are in danger here. Let's just get on with the job, please?"

"Right, Lorne, you take the back. Sir, if you'll go round the side of the building, see if there are any possible escape routes there? And I'll see what I can find out here. I don't have to tell you to stay alert at all times. Call out if you sense any danger, okay?"

"Okay," Lorne said before she took off. Keeping low, she snuck past the side window. She surveyed the area from the shelter of the house. Two huge barns lay just beyond the driveway at the rear. Still no car in sight. Lorne crouched and ran across the driveway, keeping to the grassy verge as much as she could while avoiding crunching along the gravel. She dipped around the side of one of the barns, out of view from the back of the house, and located Felicity's car. Instead of reporting her findings to Katy, she ventured farther and inspected the other barn, which was smaller than the first. After squeezing through a panel in the side, she rifled through a pile of fabric in the corner. Nothing in the pile indicated that any of the material was old. But all the clothes belonged to men, raising her suspicions that the abducted men were either dead or being kept naked somewhere in the vicinity. After searching the barn, Lorne concluded that she should get back to the house and apprise Katy and Sean of what she'd found. As she left the barn, she heard raised voices, a man crying out in pain, then silence again. She bolted back to the house to find Katy peering through a downstairs window.

Out of breath, Lorne joined her. "She's here, all right. Her car's in the barn."

"Great. Where's Roberts?" Katy asked.

"He should have returned by now. Maybe he's made his way back to the car, unless…"

"Unless what?" Katy urged.

"I heard a man cry out in pain. You don't think… he's been abducted, do you?"

CHAPTER SIXTEEN

"No. She wouldn't, would she?"

Lorne swept a hand over her face. "Shit, shit, shit! I knew we should have called for backup."

"All right, Lorne. I'll place the call now. Keep watch for me."

Lorne looked left and right constantly, her ears pricked for any noise, while Katy contacted the station. She hit her thigh as she thought about Sean's obvious cry for help. Instinct told her she should have immediately searched for the source of the noise. "Be safe, Sean. We're coming to get you."

Katy hung up. "Fuck. There's something major going on, a hostage situation in London, and all the armed response teams are on standby for that. I've pleaded with them to send a small team over ASAP, but I don't hold out much hope of them arriving anytime soon. Looks like this is down to you and me, hon."

"No way. Is the station sending out any uniforms to help us?"

"I think so. Again they're busy, but they've promised me they're going to try and jiggle things around a bit."

"Mind if I make a suggestion in that case?" Lorne raced, grasping for a solution. They obviously couldn't go in by themselves for fear of further endangering Sean's life.

"Shoot! I'm open to just about anything right now."

"Let me ring Tony. He's used to situations like this."

"What are we, about thirty minutes from your place?"

"Yeah, about thirty. I think it's our only option. They could be armed up to the hilt in there for all we know." Lorne took her mobile out of her pocket and dialled home. "Tony. We need your help."

"In what way, love?"

"We've located a suspect for the case we're working and staking the place out now. The thing is, we think this woman has just abducted Sean."

"What? Sean Roberts?"

"Yep, he decided he fancied a trip out in the field for a change. He must have let his guard down. We weren't sure if the suspect was at the location or not."

"Damn! What can I do?"

"Backup is a bit thin on the ground, some major event kicking off in the city. I wondered if you wanted to join in the fun here?"

"You bet."

"I'm sure Charlie will be all right there. Just to be on the safe side, give Carol a call, ask her to drop by and sit with her. Tony, I've got to go."

"I'll organise things here. Where are you?"

Lorne hurriedly told him the address and hung up. "He'll be here as soon as he can."

"Yeah, okay. And in the meantime, we just sit and wait?"

"It would be best. Nothing stopping us from snooping around out the back, though, is there?"

"I wonder if this Felicity thinks Sean is alone or has come out here as part of a team?"

"Who knows? Want to make a bet that he drops us in it?"

"You underestimate him, Katy. He's more savvy than you give him credit for, I assure you."

"Yeah, I guess you don't get to be a DCI without some nous. Sorry, I don't mean to be disrespectful of one of your friends, but I've seen very little of his leadership skills since my promotion."

"Er... I'm always available to share problems with. However, now is neither the time nor the place, Katy."

Her partner slapped her forehead with the palm of her hand. "Okay, let's make a move. It'll be best if we stick together."

Lorne nodded and followed Katy in a crouching position around to the back of the property. She indicated the location of the car and the other barn where she'd found the clothes.

"Let's see what else we can find, shall we?" Katy said.

Apart from the odd half tin of paint, even upstairs on the mezzanine level, they found nothing. No signs of movement came from inside the house, either.

"We need a strategy, a what-if plan of action," Lorne suggested.

They crouched by the door to the barn to observe the house.

Katy sighed. "Granted, but without backup, it's going to be tough. I say we hang out here for now, at least until Tony gets here, then we can decide the best course of action. At the moment, I'm at a loss to know what to do next without putting Sean in jeopardy."

* * *

Felicity had mixed feelings about holding the latest man hostage. He could deny it all he liked, nevertheless, he was obviously a copper. *Why else would he be out here?* He claimed he'd taken a wrong turn and was searching for someone to give him instructions back to the main road, but that just didn't cut it with her. Maybe a little punishment would help loosen his tongue. She thought it best to keep him away from the other men, although there was very little space to house him separately.

Mags had spotted the intruder outside while putting out the rubbish. She'd immediately reported back to Felicity that she'd seen a man sneaking around the side of the house. With the cattle prod she'd just used on Jordan still in her hand, Felicity pounced on the stranger when his back was turned. The element of surprise and the poke in the rear with the cattle prod had caused the man to cry out. Mags and Kaz had knocked him out with the bars they were carrying, caught him before he hit the ground, and dragged him through the back door. Now, he was lying prostrate on the stone floor of the kitchen.

"Let's get his hands and feet secured, ladies."

"We should move him first, shouldn't we, Felicity?" Mags asked.

"Yes, but where to? I don't want him with the other men."

"Why?" Kaz frowned.

"What if he's a copper?" Felicity retorted.

"Well, if you think that, why are you holding him in the first place?"

"Good point. Okay, let's drag him into the room where the other men are. Actually, before you do that, I need to knock Jordan out. I have something extra special planned for him later. I'll be right back. If that one comes round, just whack him over the head with something." Felicity left the kitchen and went to find her handbag. She extracted the syringe with the knockout drug and approached the totally exhausted Jordan. He seemed submissive, for a change, but she injected him all the same. Within seconds, he was unconscious.

Felicity unlocked the stocks restraining Jordan, then Mags and Kaz helped her put the new arrival's feet and hands into the grooves and clamped the stocks shut again.

"That'll be a nice surprise when he wakes up. Hopefully, it'll teach him not to poke his nose in where it's not wanted. Help me get this one onto the altar. Come on, girls, lend a hand. He's a dead weight." *He'll just be* dead *when I've finished with him.*

"What do you intend doing to him?" David asked, his voice quaking with fear.

"Keep quiet, or I swear, you'll be next," Felicity warned.

The man's gulp bounced off the stone walls as the women carried Jordan into the next room, placed his body on the stone altar, and put his hands and feet in the cuffs attached to the stone table.

"There, he won't get out of that. Let's see if any of the other men have changed their minds about signing over what you ladies are owed yet."

The group returned to the room where the other men were captive. Felicity revelled in the shock and apprehension written on their faces. The newcomer was beginning to stir. *He'll wait.* Transferring Jordan out of the room proved to be an ingenious stroke by Felicity. As soon as she approached the other men, they willingly signed the documents necessary to stave off any further torture, much to Felicity's amusement. The devil inside her was determined to keep striking fear in the men despite their cooperation, and she approached David with a smirk on her face, the cattle prod in her hand.

His scream startled the newcomer into life.

"What the? Stop that." He glanced down at his restrained hands and feet then looked up at Felicity. "What the hell is going on here? Some form of witchcraft? Release me at once."

"Ah, our new guest is awake. Missing out on the fun, are you, dear? Take that." She sharply prodded his bare midriff, and he cried out.

"You can't do this. I'm a detective chief inspector in the Met."

Felicity tilted her head back and laughed as the other women in the group gasped. "A DCI, nonetheless. How nice of you to join us. Are you alone?"

"Yes."

"And what, pray tell me, is a DCI doing out in the wilderness?"

"I was lost. I stopped to ask the way. I didn't envisage being stripped and trussed up like this. Let me go now, and I promise not to take any personal action against you."

"Personal action against me? Meaning what?"

"Meaning that you'll have abduction charges brought against you for what you've done to these men, but as far as I'm concerned, I'd be willing to drop all charges, *only* if you let me go now."

"I'm sorry. That's just not going to happen. I'm not letting anyone go, not tonight, not ever. The lot of you will be punished for how you treat women, even you." She pointed at the police officer.

"I bet you've been guiltier than most for treating women abhorrently in your role. It goes with the territory, doesn't it? Exert your manly power, and the women fall into line or get demoted and kicked out of the force. Am I right?"

"No. I've always treated women fairly."

Felicity noticed a faint grimace when he spoke. She stepped forward a few steps and waved the prod in his face. "Truth or consequences?"

The copper closed his eyes in defeat as if he'd been rumbled. "All right, I guess I'm guilty of exerting my male dominance or trying to, over the female members of my staff, but it has always been done without intention, and I've regretted my actions immediately."

"Poppycock! What kind of idiot do you take me for?" She jabbed him, and this time, left the metal against his skin for a few more seconds.

The officer twisted this way and that as again he cried out. Then the pain overwhelmed him, and he fell unconscious.

CHAPTER SEVENTEEN

"Oh my God, are my ears deceiving me, or did I just hear a man cry out, scream even?" Lorne strained her ear towards the house.

"Not deceiving you at all. I'd say that it sounded like Sean. I could be imagining it, though."

"I hope you're wrong. There's Tony. Let me get his attention." Lorne picked up a stone and hurled it at a patch of ground near Tony's feet. He looked up, and she motioned for him to join them in the barn. After giving him a brief hug, she filled him in on what they knew so far. "So, we've got to find a way of getting in there, quickly, Tony."

"It's going to be tricky without the necessary backup. We should get in there soon if you think you heard Sean crying out. Let me do a quick reccy of the area, and then we'll decide what to do for the best."

Before Lorne could stop him, he took off towards the house. He peered through the windows then disappeared around the side elevation of the house. He returned moments later, looking thoughtful.

"Anything?" Lorne asked eagerly.

"As far as I can see, there are three possible ways in. The front and back doors and a kind of trapdoor around that side, which I'm presuming is the way into a cellar."

"Trouble with that scenario is that any likely activity is probably taking place in the cellar. We want to surprise them if we decide to make a move before backup arrives," Lorne pointed out.

"I agree. The cries we heard seemed very distant, like they came from deep within the house. What do you suggest, Tony, using your experience in similar situations?"

He puffed out his cheeks. "I'm not sure, to be honest. For a start, I'm usually loaded up with weapons." He held up his empty hands. "Also, I generally have an indication what I'm dealing with. Intel on how many people are involved, maybe schematics of the property."

"Ha, spoken like a true MI6 operative. Hey, welcome to our world, hon. Most of the time, we have to go into these kinds of situations empty-handed and unsure of our surroundings." Lorne grinned and tweaked his cheek.

"That'd be ex-MI6 operative with a bum leg, to boot, dear wife."

"All right, we don't have time for a domestic. We need to come up with a plan and pretty damn quick if we want to get Sean—and the other men, of course—out of there soon," Katy said.

Lorne shrugged. "Apart from each of us taking one of the ways into the property and hoping for the best that one of us gets to Sean before something drastic happens to him, I'm at a loss how to proceed."

Katy took her mobile out of her pocket and walked to the back of the barn.

"What do you think she's doing?" Tony asked.

"My guess is she's chasing up the ART unit. Time is of the essence, after all. Everything all right at home?"

"Yeah, Carol turned up just as I was leaving. She looked grim but didn't enlighten me as to why."

"Crap, that doesn't bode well for us then," Lorne said as Katy returned.

"What doesn't bode well? … oh, never mind. There's a team on the way. Funny how things can change and rise to the top of the urgent list when a DCI's life is in peril."

"How long? Any idea?" Lorne asked, pleased that things were at last looking up.

"Half an hour to an hour—they couldn't be more specific than that," Katy replied sullenly.

"If we have that long," Tony grumbled.

"Don't say that, Tony," Lorne said, biting her bottom lip. "Do you think we should get in there without waiting for backup?"

Tony shrugged. "If I was in charge, that's what I'd be doing. It's Katy's call, though."

"Shit! Thanks, guys. Let me weigh up our options. Sean cries out in pain, and we're expected to wait it out until the cavalry arrives. Or we charge the building, screw up big time, and face the wrath of our superiors. Jesus!"

"That's the hand we've been dealt, Katy. I know what I would do if I were still a DI," Lorne stated.

Katy glared at her. "I know full well what you would do, Lorne Warner—you'd rush the joint and suffer the consequences from the super later, wouldn't you?"

Lorne grinned. "Yep. We have extra manpower, don't forget, Katy. It's your call, though."

Tony sniggered, and Lorne jabbed her elbow in his ribs.

"Crap, crap, crap. Okay, Tony, I'm counting on you to guide us on this one, okay?"

"Go, Katy!" Lorne high-fived her partner and her husband.

"Let's leave the celebrations until the mission has been completed, shall we? So, Tony, it's over to you."

Before Tony could open his mouth to speak, another man's scream rang out from the house.

"Jesus, we better get in there ASAP. Are you girls up for the fight? Can we search around for possible weapons? We can't go in empty-handed. There's no telling what we'll be confronted with when we get in there."

They picked out several gardening tools they found around the barn: a hoe, a rake, anything with a long handle able to swipe and disarm an attacker.

"Hey, I've found this. Any good?" Lorne pointed at the weed-killing sprayer in the corner.

"Is there any weed-killer solution with it?" Tony asked.

Katy opened the lids to a few nearby boxes. "I think I've found it. All we need now is water."

Lorne ran out of the barn and returned carrying a bucket of water. "There was a water butt outside. I noticed it on the way in. Looks like we're in business. If we spray it in folk's eyes, it'll buy us some time to search for Sean when we're inside."

Tony filled the container with the weed killer and topped it up with water from the bucket. "Great idea. I'll dilute the solution a little—I'd hate to cause any permanent damage. It is women we're dealing with here, after all. Are we ready, ladies? Lorne, do you want to go first with the spray?"

Lorne shook her head at her husband's underestimating the power of a woman in this situation. She'd met several determined and evil female suspects over the years who could show their male counterparts a thing or two, but they didn't have time for a gender war of words—Sean's life was in danger. "Nothing would give me greater pleasure. Shall we go through the back door, if it's open, that is?"

"That's what I'm thinking," Tony said.

They ran across the yard, not bothering to conceal their presence. Reaching the back door, Tony turned the handle and pulled a surprised face when he found it unlocked.

"I think they're expecting us." He pushed open the door, and Lorne ran into an antiquated kitchen.

A woman screamed out and ran at them. Lorne aimed the solution at the woman's face. She took a direct hit and crumpled to the floor, screaming, "You've blinded me!"

Lorne, Katy, and Tony bolted past her and headed for the cellar. A strange noise originated from the depths of the house.

"It sounds like someone chanting," Katy said from the rear.

Tony yanked open the door. Again, Lorne was ready to use the solution, but the stairwell was clear. Gingerly, they walked down the steps. The chanting grew louder the nearer they got to the bottom.

Tony pointed at a door where the voices seemed to be coming from. "The coast appears to be clear. We need to get in there."

"How? We're going to have to barge in, catch them unawares…" Katy began before a woman's scream sounded at the top of the stairs.

"Intruders. Help me. We've got intruders!"

The door flew open, and the two detectives and Tony sprinted towards it without consulting each other. Tony struggled to fend off the woman coming at him with an axe raised above her head. Lorne reacted swiftly and squirted the woman's eyes. The advancing woman dropped her weapon and screamed in agony, scratching at her eyes.

Tony, Lorne, and Katy ran through the open doorway and stopped dead in their tracks at the image before them. Lying on a stone altar was an unconscious naked man. A group of women wearing black cloaks surrounded him, each staring at the intruders.

The leader grabbed something off the table behind her, raised it above her head, and angled it over the man. It was a long-bladed knife. "Come any closer, and he gets it."

Lorne exchanged a questioning look with Katy and Tony, asking what to do next. While they were deciding, a confrontation kicked off between two of the women in the room, and one of them threw herself over the man's body.

"I won't let you sacrifice him. Jordan, I love you. Please forgive me."

The leader tugged at the woman shielding the man. "Get off him, Dara. He needs to die for what he's done to you. Let me do this— you won't regret it."

"You'll have to kill us both then. I'm not moving. Won't you girls help me? She's lost her mind. She's trying to control all of us, making us do things against our will. I won't let her get away with this."

While the leader was distracted, bent on venting her anger on the woman and the man on the altar, Lorne, Katy and Tony charged at her without thinking of their own safety. She swung the blade in their direction. Tony grabbed the woman around the neck, subjecting her to a sleeper hold. The woman went limp in his arms.

"All right, ladies. Your little game is over."

Boots thundered down the steps of the cellar, and a bunch of shouting, armed men entered the room, instructing everyone to get down on the floor.

"Cuff them all," the leader of the Armed Response Team shouted.

Lorne and Katy quickly produced their IDs and claimed Tony as their associate. The man in charge identified himself and asked if anyone was hurt.

"No, we're fine. Somewhere around here, we believe they're holding a group of men," Tony told him.

Lorne knelt next to one of the women on the floor. "The men, where are they?"

The woman said nothing, but her eyes drifted off to the left.

Lorne and Katy barged through the door to the adjacent room. They travelled down the length of a line of men towards Sean Roberts.

"Help us, please?" several of the petrified men shouted as they ran past.

"You're safe now. Bear with us," Katy told them.

Lorne swept up a cloth sack as she passed and threw it over Sean's private area as she approached him. Bending down, she gently touched his face while searching for a pulse at his neck with her other hand. "Sean, Sean, can you hear me?" Feeling a faint pulse, she shook him and begged him to open his eyes. "His pulse is weak, Katy, call an ambulance."

EPILOGUE

A few days later, Lorne decided everyone could do with cheering up, so she invited all of those involved in the latest case they'd cracked to attend a barbecue at the rescue centre.

As Lorne carried the steaks out to Tony, a very eager Carol joined her, keen to hear what had happened to the woman she'd had a bad feeling about. "Don't keep me in suspense any longer, Lorne, please?"

She shrugged. "It's not intentional, Carol. I really don't have much to tell. The woman is pleading insanity. She's undergoing tests at present to see if she's well enough to go to court to face charges of abducting and torturing the men."

"Wow, really?" Carol leaned in and whispered, "She's cute, that one, far from insane."

"Yeah, that much I've worked out already. She'll slip up during the examination. I have no doubts about that—people always do when falsely waving the insanity card to hide their true motivations for carrying out heinous crimes such as this."

"Has she given any clues at all as to why she did it?" Carol asked, setting a salad bowl on the table next to the plates and glasses.

"Nope, although the other women were quick to apportion the blame in her ex-husband's direction. Apparently, he traded her in for a younger model, and instead of accepting his decision and moving on with her life, she vowed to get revenge when the opportunity arose."

"I take it one of the abducted men was her husband then?"

"Nope, don't you find that bizarre?" Lorne handed the steaks to Tony. Her husband grabbed her wrist and pulled her to him for a kiss.

"Get a room, you two," Charlie shouted from the paddock.

"That is kind of perplexing," Carol replied thoughtfully.

"Maybe she was practicing, perfecting her skills to cause her ex maximum damage when she finally confronted him," Tony suggested. He pressed each steak in turn with the tongs so the juice ran out and made the flames leap up to sear the meat.

Lorne nodded. "I hadn't really thought of that, love. You could be right."

"Anyway, I'm glad it all turned out well in the end. How is Sean now?" Carol asked.

"Nothing really hurt, except his male pride. That'll teach him to try and wind Katy up and vacate his desk in search of some real police action, won't it?" Lorne laughed, knowing she wasn't saying anything that she wouldn't say to her boss's face.

Katy and AJ joined the group, holding hands.

Lorne slung an arm around Katy's shoulder and pecked her rosy cheek. "I'm glad you two have decided to come out in the open. Any idea what's going to happen about work?"

The couple smiled adoringly at each other and shook their heads. Katy tried to explain the situation the best she could. "I've discussed the matter with Roberts, and he seems to think AJ can continue working with the team until a vacancy in a different department crops up. Of course, that could take months yet, so Roberts advised us to keep a low profile at work. You know, not to tout it around just in case anyone higher up the ladder witnesses anything untoward and makes a formal complaint about us."

"He has a point, I guess. Is Sean coming today? He was undecided whether or not he'd make it out of hospital in time the last I spoke to him," Lorne said.

"He said he was coming. There he is now, looking rather sheepish, if you ask me. His wife seems nice, far prettier than I thought she'd be."

"Katy! Leave her alone. She's never done you any harm," Lorne smiled and took off to welcome Sean and his wife to the gathering. "Glad you could make it. Where's the baby?"

"Typical copper," Sean complained, "asking questions before dishing out the drinks. If you must know, little Sara is at home with the mother-in-law."

"Never mind. Glad you could both join us. How are you feeling now, Sean?"

"I'll be back to work on Monday, as the doc suggested. Don't tell me you've missed me, Lorne? That'd be a first."

Lorne winked at his wife. "I've been busy setting up a torture room at the station. We women coppers have obviously been getting it wrong all these years. We could learn a thing or two from the witches. It's one way of keeping you men in line anyway."

"Dinner up, come and get it," Tony shouted in the nick of time.

"Saved by the bell again. Aren't I the lucky one?" Sean replied with a smile laced with sarcasm.

Lorne looked over at her husband and smiled. "I'll be there in a mo…"

The crowd quietened down, then the air filled with oohs and aahs when Charlie and Carol approached the group with Onyx. The boxer strode confidently alongside Charlie and glanced back at the pups running to keep up with her.

Lorne whistled. "Nice outfit."

"Do you think so?" Carol said, puffing out her chest and fiddling with the colourful quilted coat covering Onyx's improving but still badly conditioned skin.

"Yep, very stylish. I can see she's going to be a very spoilt little doggy when she finally ends up living with you, Carol."

"There was never any doubt, was there? Now all we have to do is decide what we're going to do with her offspring."

"No. I forbid you having them," Lorne chastised her friend good-naturedly. She had a feeling her words would fall on deaf ears.

Carol bent down to pet the dog that was now wagging her tail freely. Then the dog lifted her ear. "We'll have to see about that. Won't we, dear?"

The crowd laughed, and Lorne shook her head. "She's impossible, isn't she?" She let out a satisfied sigh, knowing that Onyx and her pups were going to the best home possible.

Note to the reader.

Thank you for reading Tortured Justice; I sincerely hope you enjoyed reading this novel as much as I loved writing it.

If you liked it, please consider posting a short review as genuine feedback is what makes all the lonely hours writers spend producing their work worthwhile.

ABOUT THE AUTHOR

New York Times, USA Today, Amazon Top 20 bestselling author, iBooks top 5 bestselling and #2 bestselling author on Barnes and Noble. I am a British author who moved to France in 2002, and that's when I turned my hobby into a career.

I share my home with two crazy dogs that like nothing better than to drag their masterful leader (that's me) around the village.

When I'm not pounding the keys of my computer keyboard I enjoy DIY, reading, gardening and painting.

14819190R00081

Printed in Great Britain
by Amazon.co.uk, Ltd.,
Marston Gate.